A LOVE THAT KNOWS NO BOUNDS

Men of Valor
Book Two

By Laura Landon

ARE YOU SIGNED UP FOR DRAGONBLADE'S BLOG?

You'll get the latest news and information on exclusive giveaways, exclusive excerpts, coming releases, sales, free books, cover reveals and more.

Check out our complete list of authors, too!

No spam, no junk. That's a promise!

Sign Up Here

www.dragonbladepublishing.com

Dearest Reader;

Thank you for your support of a small press. At Dragonblade Publishing, we strive to bring you the highest quality Historical Romance from some of the best authors in the business. Without your support, there is no 'us', so we sincerely hope you adore these stories and find some new favorite authors along the way.

Happy Reading!

CEO, Dragonblade Publishing

Additional Dragonblade books by Author Laura Landon

Men of Valor Series
A Love For All Time (Book 1)
A Love That Knows No Bounds (Book 2)

CHAPTER ONE

OLIVIA MATTHEWS MADE her way down the stairs from the nursery on the third floor with a basket of laundry in her hands. She dropped the clothes off, then headed for the side entrance of The Angel's Wings Orphanage and Foundling Home. The kitchen exit was the shortest path that led to her cottage.

As supervisor of the orphanage and foundling home, most nights Livie was forced to stay at the orphanage, but on those rare occasions when she needed to get away, she went to the cottage the orphanage provided so she could get some uninterrupted sleep. Unfortunately, she didn't get to stay there often enough.

Between helping new mothers birth their infants, and caring for them when they were born, then searching for parents who were willing to adopt them, there weren't enough hours in the day to see to the running of the orphanage. It was a full-time job and Livie dreamed of the day when she had someone to help her.

For today though, Livie couldn't wait to get home and crawl into bed. She couldn't wait to finally get a few hours of much-needed sleep. She'd hardly slept for the past two nights, what with one of the expectant mothers giving birth and one of the newborns running a fever. Just when she thought things would calm down, several of the children woke with nightmares. It had been one catastrophe after another.

The back stairs led directly to the kitchen and the smells

coming from the bread and pastries Mrs. Barnes was baking caused Livie's stomach to growl from hunger. She couldn't remember the last time she'd eaten. It had to have been at least a day or longer ago.

Livie stepped into the kitchen and took the pastry Mrs. Barnes handed her.

"Thank you, Mrs. Barnes."

"Are you finally going home, Mrs. Matthews?" Mrs. Barnes asked as Livie made her way through the kitchen.

"Yes. I'm more tired than usual so I'm going to leave early."

"You should be tired, Mrs. Matthews. The girls tell me you stayed up all night with the lass birthing her babe two nights ago, then with little Timmy last night. Is the lad better?"

"Yes," Livie answered on a sigh. "At least he's no longer running a fever. He gave me a fright though during the night."

"Mandy said you were afraid he wouldn't make it."

"He still has a way to go, but I think he'll make it now."

"If he does, he'll have you to thank."

"Not me, Mrs. Barnes. God was watching over him. He gets all the credit."

"That He does. Now, you go home and get a good night's sleep," Mrs. Barnes said, helping Livie with her wrap. "And don't come tomorrow until afternoon. Little Timmy will be fine and if he takes a turn for the worse, we'll send someone for you."

"Promise?"

"I promise. Now go home and rest. We can't afford for you to get ill. The orphanage would fall apart if you did."

Livie laughed at the compliment, but knew that was hardly true. If she'd learned anything from her father, it was that no one was irreplaceable. No one was that important. And, she'd learned that lesson the hard way.

Livie took a bite of her pastry, then continued on her way. She didn't think she'd ever been so tired in her life. Timmy had been the third of four additions to the orphanage in the past five days, and it had taken all of Livie's time and energy to get the babe settled. Livie couldn't remember a time when there had been this many orphans to care for at The Angel's Wings or a time when the orphanage had been this short-staffed. One of the first things Livie intended to do when she had time was hire at least one additional staff member to care for the overabundance of children. Even if she had to pay them out of her own pocket.

Livie fastened the frogs on her wrap and stepped out into the brisk night air. Spring wouldn't be here for at least a month or more and the dead of winter still had a firm grip on this part of northern England. Livie couldn't wait until the new season made an appearance.

Livie pulled the hood of her wrap over her head and headed for home. She didn't live far from the orphanage, but she was so exhausted tonight her cottage seemed far away indeed. Livie lowered her head and walked in the direction of her cottage.

She hadn't gone far when she heard a low moaning sound. Her feet came to a halt.

She wasn't sure what had caused the sound, but her first thought was that the low guttural moan had come from a wounded animal. She paused to listen.

She heard the keening sound again and turned. Whatever it was seemed to be behind a clump of trees to her right.

Livie took one step closer toward the sound, then another. Her boots crunched atop the frozen snow and a twig snapped beneath her foot. She stopped short and the sound made from the injured animal or human quieted.

It was impossible to see clearly because of the shade that blanketed the area, but when she took another step into the clearing, her sight improved.

That's when she saw it.

A form lay on the ground. It was too big to be an animal and when it moved, Livie realized it was a human. The form stilled as if trying to escape her notice, but all it accomplished was to moan again.

She stepped closer to where the form huddled in the snow.

That's when she noticed the blood-soaked snow surrounding his body.

"Lay still," she whispered, stepping closer to him. She knelt at his side and pressed her hand against his chest where a bullet had entered. "You're injured."

The man was more than injured. He was dying.

"I need to get you to shelter," she whispered, brushing the hair from his brow. "But you'll have to help me. I'll take you back to the orphanage."

"No," he answered in a weak, raspy voice. "No time. Here."

The man reached for Livie's hand and pressed some papers and a cold, hard object into her palm. "Hide these," he whispered, wrapping her fingers around the objects.

"What are they?"

"That doesn't... matter. Don't give them... to anyone but... Jason."

"Jason, who?"

"Jason... do you hear?"

"Yes," Livie answered. "Only give them to Jason."

"Promise... me," he rasped.

"I promise, but I don't know a Jason. What does he look like?"

"Dark hair... and he has a... scar across his... forehead. His name is... Jason. Jason."

"I promise. I'll only give these to Jason."

"Tell him... to find... the traitor..." he gasped. "He can't trust... anyone."

"Yes. I'll tell him."

"You can't trust... anyone. Promise you... won't."

"I promise. I won't trust anyone except Jason."

"Bless... you," he whispered, then closed his eyes and took his last breath.

Livie held the man's hand long after he was gone. There was something compelling about the desperation in his words, as if his request held the most vital importance.

She clutched the items he'd given her and held them close. Whatever he'd given her had significant value. It had cost the man before her his life.

CHAPTER TWO

LIVIE SAT BEHIND her desk and studied the account ledgers. No matter how many times she went over the numbers, the outlook remained the same – there wasn't enough money to adequately feed and clothe the children for another month, let alone through spring and into summer. They'd have to watch every penny they spent and budget wisely.

The weight resting on Livie's shoulders seemed heavier than usual. She placed her pen on the desk and closed the ledger she'd been working on. This wasn't the first time money had been in short supply. It was simply that the need was greater this year than she remembered it ever being before. There were more women and children who needed rescuing than usual. And the number of supporters for the orphanage seemed fewer.

If only she could find a way to add to their income.

If only she could think of something she could do to make some money to take care of the children.

She leaned back in her chair and rested her chin on her steepled fingers. She'd been at The Angel's Wings for nearly five years and each year it was more difficult to make ends meet. She was going to have to find additional ways to provide an income for the orphanage. Additional ways to make money for the foundling home. And yet, very few of the young women who came here to have their children had any money to give them.

How could they demand something that none of them had?

A knock on the door brought Livie out of her musings. "Yes."

"You have a caller, Mrs. Matthews," Marie announced when she entered the room.

"Who is it, Marie?"

"There's a Theodore Dunworthy to see you, ma'am. I believe he's here in search of work."

Livie shook her head. "Tell him we can't afford to hire another staff member, Marie. Have Mrs. Barnes feed him and send him on his way."

"Very well, Mrs. Matthews." Marie bobbed respectfully, then left the room. It was less than a minute before Marie tapped on the door and entered the room again.

"Yes, Marie?"

"The man refuses to leave, Mrs. Matthews. He says he wants no pay. He says he's satisfied to work for nothing more than food and a bed in which to sleep."

Livie sat forward in her chair and considered what the man offered.

"He's a fine looking man, ma'am. Big enough he appears he could do a full day's work and more. And with winter looking like it isn't going away anytime soon, there's a need for more firewood than Frank can keep up with."

Livie considered what Marie said. Frank had been the handyman at the orphanage for going on forty years and his age, plus the increase of children to care for, were taking a toll on his time as well as his health. Maybe it wouldn't be such a hardship to feed and house another handyman at least until spring. It could be that this man was the answer to her prayers.

"Show him in, Marie. I'll see if I think he'll fill the post."

"Yes, ma'am." Marie turned and left the room, then returned with the man on her heels.

"Mr. Theodore Dunworthy, Mrs. Matthews."

"Thank you, Marie." Livie stood behind her desk and lifted her gaze as the tall, imposing man entered the room.

Her gaze locked with the man introduced as Theodore Dunworthy and her breath caught. The blood drained from her face and her legs trembled so violently she had to grab hold of the desk to keep her balance.

This couldn't be happening. It couldn't be. It was impossible.

Livie's legs threatened to give out beneath her, and she clutched her grip on the desk even tighter to stay on her feet.

"Get out!" she ordered in a threatening growl as she glared at the man's dark hair and familiar midnight blue eyes. She rushed across the room and threw open the door. "You heard me! Get out!"

The man before her seemed larger than she remembered. He seemed taller and his shoulders appeared broader. Olivia felt smaller, more fragile, than she'd been the last time she'd seen him.

Livie swallowed hard to take in a breath and glared at the man standing before her. "Get out, Theo! Get the hell out of here!"

She stared in disbelief at the man she hadn't seen for nearly five years, then hardened her gaze to a hostile glare. He wasn't a ghost. He was the last person in the world she wanted to see.

This was the man who'd destroyed her life, then abandoned her. She'd hoped to never see him again in this life or the next. Yet, here he was. Standing before her as if he had a right to be here.

Olivia prayed it was possible he hadn't recognized her, but from the wide-eyed look of surprise on his face he was as shocked by her presence as she was by his.

"Get out, Theo," she repeated. "Now!"

"Livie," he started to say, but Livie couldn't allow him to spend even one second in her presence. She couldn't risk letting him discover anything about her, or what she'd done or gone through over the last five years. She couldn't allow him to have anything to do with her. He'd destroyed her life once and she refused to allow him to do it again.

"You heard me! Get out!" Livie stepped around him and threw open the door. "Get out!"

"Please," he said. "Just listen to me. I need your help. I'm desperate."

"So am I," she countered. "I'm desperate for you to get out of my sight. I want you gone. I never want to see you again."

He reached out and closed the door His movement put him in too close a proximity to her.

"I know you don't, Livie. But please. Just hear me out."

"No! I don't want to hear anything you have to say."

"I know I owe you an apology. I should have at least said goodbye before I left. But—"

"Yes, that's the least you could have done. But it's too late now. I don't want to hear any of your excuses. I don't want to hear anything you have to say."

"Livie, please."

Livie looked at the man she'd loved all those years ago and her heart clenched in her breast. He still had the power to cause tumult to rage inside her. Still had the ability to affect her like no other man ever could.

She turned her head. She didn't want to look at him. She couldn't allow him to get anywhere close to her. Not after he'd hurt her like he had.

She focused on him. If anything, he was even taller and more muscular than he'd been the last time she'd seen him. His massive physique cast a long shadow that stretched far into the room, and his broad shoulders made the room seem smaller. His formidable stance caused Livie to stare in awe at his presence.

But it wasn't only his physical appearance that seemed so different and caused her breath to catch in her throat. It was his eyes. Livie found herself mesmerized by the startling midnight blue of his gaze. When he looked at her, she felt as though he had the power to capture her and hold her in his grasp. Just like he'd done before.

But the man standing before her had changed from the man

he'd been before he left for the war. The look in his eyes told her he'd seen things that had affected him. Things that had changed him.

And he'd been injured. A scar ran the length of his face, from his hairline, down his temple and his cheek to beneath his jaw.

The mark should have made him terrifying and ugly. Even frightening. Instead, it gave him a piratical appearance. A roguish look that caused him to appear even more threatening.

Livie studied the scar that marred his perfection and realized that all she wanted to do was cup her hand to his cheek and comfort him for the pain he'd endured.

"I'm not going to tell you again, Theo. Leave!"

"I can't, Livie."

Livie didn't want to argue with him. She didn't want to fight with him. She just wanted him to go. She turned her back to him and stepped to the window behind her desk.

Snow had started falling and if he didn't leave soon, it wouldn't be safe to send him away. "Please, Theo. Leave."

"I can't, Livie. I need your help."

"I can't help you. We can't take on another staff member. I have no funds to pay you."

"I don't need to be paid. I only need to be fed and given a bed in which to sleep. I'll work for my keep."

Livie kept her back to him and stared out the window. "What are you doing here?" she asked as she stared at the large flakes floating down and blanketing the earth.

"I'm just passing through. I'm traveling to London."

"Are you still in the army?"

"No. I got out when the war was over."

"Why are you known as Theodore Dunworthy?"

"I took my mother's name when I entered the service."

"Why?"

"I didn't want to be known by my father's name. There was too much to live up to with that name. And, I didn't want my father to find me."

Livie considered what Theo meant by that statement. Captain Theodore Hamilton would have been labeled a war hero and London Society wouldn't have let him live in peace.

Livie remembered reading about Captain Dunworthy and a group of his fellow soldiers. They had single-handedly saved hundreds of lives by infiltrating behind enemy lines and retrieving enemy battle plans. They'd been written about in every newspaper in London and lauded as true.

Captain Theodore *Hamilton* was a war hero who would have drawn attention wherever he went. The Theo she knew would have hated such attention, especially looking as he did now, with a scar that ran the length of his face and had changed his features so drastically.

"Let me stay here, Livie. The stable will be fine. A barn. Just for a while. Just until I get back on my feet. Please."

Livie considered her options. How could she force him back outside in such inclement weather without at least giving him a meal? And how could she turn him away when she needed his help so desperately? There was so much that needed to be done. So much good he could do here. But the risks were so great. What if he discovered what she was hiding? What if he found out what had brought her here?

"Livie, please. Don't turn me away. Let me stay for at least a few nights. Please."

Livie lowered her head and rested her forehead against the cold windowpane. Finally, she pushed herself away from the glass and turned to face him. "Just for a few days, Theo. Just until you get back on your feet."

"Thank you, Livie. You won't regret it."

"I already do, Theo, and you know why."

"Things won't be like they were before. I promise."

"No, they won't. Nothing will be like it was before. I'm older now. I'm not nearly the fool I was then."

She narrowed her glare to prove the sincerity of her words. She wasn't the fool she'd been five years ago.

She'd learned her lesson. She was much wiser now.

She wouldn't let him make a fool of her now like he'd done before.

"Marie," she called out when she opened the door. "Show Captain Dunworthy to a room, then take him to the kitchen and have Mrs. Barnes give him something to eat. In the morning take him to Frank." She turned her attention to Theo. "You'll report to Frank in the morning. He'll tell you what needs to be done. I don't want to see you again. Do you understand?"

"Yes, Livie. Thank you," he said.

"It's Mrs. Matthews."

"You're married?"

"Yes."

"Good. I'm glad. You deserve to be happy."

"Then don't forget it and stay away from me."

"Of course, Mrs. Matthews."

"Now, go."

"Yes," he answered and left the room.

The minute the door closed behind him, Livie sank into the chair behind her desk and dropped her head to her hands. Somehow, she knew she'd just made the biggest mistake of her life. As big as the mistake she'd made nearly five years ago. A mistake she was still paying for.

Chapter Three

THEO LAY IN his bed and stared at the inky darkness until his eyes started to cross. He'd tried to get to sleep all night long and failed. Finally, he threw the covers from over him and got to his feet.

What were the chances that his life would collide with Livie's after all this time? What trick was God playing on him? Of all the places in the world, why had he been sent to The Angel's Wings Foundling Home and Orphanage to meet with the agent who had retrieved papers and a jewel from the French? Why was he forced to come face-to-face with the one person on earth who haunted his dreams and refused to leave him in peace for even one minute of his life?

Theo pulled on his clothes and left his room. Of all the unlucky coincidences, meeting Livie here was the last thing he wanted to happen or expected.

Theo raked his fingers through his hair and made his way down the stairs and to the kitchen. He grabbed a day-old pastry from the counter and ate it as he walked through the door and out into the crisp morning air.

There was a pile of wood that needed to be chopped and physical exercise was exactly what he needed in order to work off his frustration. He attacked each log of wood as if it were an enemy he needed to destroy in order to atone for what he'd done to Olivia Howard nearly five years ago.

He brought the ax down and chopped the wood on the block in two. Then he repeated the process again and again and again.

If there was anything in his life that he regretted, it was walking away from her without telling her goodbye. Or not writing to her even once during the three years he fought.

He'd been such a coward. But what could he have told her?

That he loved her? That he wanted to marry her? He couldn't have told her either of those things. How could he have expected her to wait for him when he doubted he'd make it back to England alive? More than once, he'd been injured so severely he doubted he would survive to come back to her.

Theo stopped long enough to run his hand over the scar that ran down his face. The scar that made him a hideous sight. Livie was better off without him. At least, that's what he told himself.

If she was *Mrs. Matthews* like she said she was, she'd found someone to marry. He wondered what had happened to her husband. Someday he'd have to ask her about him. But not now. He wasn't ready to hear that she'd found true happiness without him.

He picked up the ax and lifted it in the air to swing at another log, then paused when a twig snapped behind him. It was barely sunup, and he didn't expect anyone to be about yet.

"How long have you been out here cutting wood?" a voice asked from behind him.

The ax halted mid-air and Theo turned to face his questioner. He knew it was Livie before he even looked at her. He'd heard her voice for years in his dreams as her soft words wrapped around him and held him close.

"I couldn't sleep. I thought I'd get an early start on the day."

He took in her presence and his heart shifted in his chest. Even though he couldn't see what she wore, he imagined it might be something as fashionable and satiny as the gown she wore the last time he'd seen her.

He imagined that beneath the hood of her cloak, her thick,

rich, auburn hair was adorned with the delicate golden daisies woven through her tresses, the same as she wore the night he'd removed them, then made love to her.

He imagined her skin was as radiant as it had been when he pulled the gown loose over her shoulders and exposed it beneath the emerald satin.

He imagined—

"Don't look at me like that, Theo," she demanded in a harsh voice.

"Like what?"

"Like you're undressing me."

"You make it difficult not to, Livie."

"Don't."

"Please, accept my apology."

"Have you spoken to Frank yet this morning?"

"No."

"He was going to fix a leak in the roof above the foyer. He'll need your help."

"Of course."

"Then, perhaps you can go to the stable and see what needs to be done there. Take Frank with you. He'll show you where the roof needs to be patched."

"Yes, Mrs. Matthews. Anything else?"

"No. Frank will tell you what's next on his list of things to do."

"Yes, ma'am."

She turned and took a few steps away from him, then stopped. "Captain Dunworthy?"

"Yes, Mrs. Matthews."

"When you decide you've stayed here long enough, please be courteous enough to inform someone that you are leaving. Unlike the last time you left me."

With those sharp words, she turned and left.

Her words stung. Mostly because they were true. More, because he deserved them. It had been cowardly of him to leave without telling her he was going, or saying goodbye. But he'd had no choice. He had to leave, or he'd never have escaped his father. And what his father had planned for him would have been a fate worse than death.

Theo finished chopping wood, then went in search of Frank. He found him on the roof above the foyer. "Mrs. Matthews sent me to help," he yelled from below.

"Good," Frank yelled down from the roof. "I need more shingles. Can you bring some up, and some nails, too?"

Theo grabbed a bundle of wooden shingles and stuffed a handful of nails into his pocket, then climbed the ladder. When he reached Frank, he climbed onto the roof and started nailing shingles to where several were missing.

"How long do you plan to stay?" Frank asked while nailing a shingle.

"I'm not sure. Probably until Mrs. Matthews tells me to go."

"Then you might be here a good long time, Captain. There's lots of work to be done here. More than I can keep up with."

"How long have you been here, Frank?"

"My whole life, it feels like. I worked here when I was a lad, and never left."

"Do you have family, Frank?"

"Yeah. My missus helps take care of the wee ones in the nursery, and my oldest two girls feed the babes. Seems like one or the other is always giving me another grandbaby, and there's always a new babe or two here who needs to be fed."

Theo smiled. "Where do all the babies come from?" Theo asked.

"From all over. Mostly, the girls who have the babes have been abandoned by the fathers and can't afford to keep their infants. Mrs. Matthews tries to find homes for each one we have, but the nearby families can only take in so many."

"How long has Mrs. Matthews been here?"

Frank hesitated as if he wasn't sure he wanted to divulge any information about Livie.

"She's been here going on five years," he answered briskly. "She came and never left. Now, hand me some of those nails you brought up."

Theo dug in his pocket and handed Frank some nails.

"You don't get many travelers passing through here, do you?"

"Can't say as we do. Why?"

"Oh, no reason. It's just that before I traveled this way, I heard from a friend I served with in the army. He mentioned that he would be traveling this way. I asked at the inn on my way here and they hadn't seen anyone matching my friend's description. Have you seen a stranger in the last week or two?"

"What's he look like?"

The expression on Frank's face turned pensive, as if Theo had brought up a subject he didn't want to talk about.

"Well, my friend's a little older than me and not quite as tall. He has brown hair and walks with a slight limp. Have you seen him?"

Frank hesitated, then shook his head. "No, I've not seen anyone like that. Maybe he decided to travel a different way."

"Yes, maybe," Theo answered, but there was something about the way Frank acted that gave Theo pause. For some reason, Frank was either hesitant to divulge any information that might be helpful, or he was lying and he had seen the agent Theo was supposed to meet. But he didn't want to let on that he'd seen him.

⊰⊱

IT HAD BEEN two weeks since Theo had arrived, and even though he'd searched several rooms in the orphanage, he hadn't found what he was looking for. Today he decided to search the attic.

Livie had left a couple of hours ago and Theo knew he could search the attic for the papers and jewel without being seen. They had to be here somewhere. He doubted she'd hide them someplace where she couldn't get to them in a hurry if she had to. Unless she hid them at the cottage where she slept when she left the orphanage. Although, that was doubtful. She was absent from her cottage too often to risk them being found when she wasn't there. There were times when she was gone from her home for days on end. He doubted Livie would be reckless enough to hide them where they could be missing for days without her realizing they were gone.

But, that was a possibility, and after he'd searched every corner of the orphanage, he'd search her cottage as a last resort.

Theo climbed the stairs and opened the door to the attic. He lit the lantern he'd brought with him and began his search. There were several trunks filled with clothes and blankets and several spare pillows. There were a few wardrobes and cradles in need of repair if they were ever to be used again. Theo thought of the rooms that were lacking cupboards and cradles and made a mental note to fix the broken furniture so it could be used.

There were some pictures and wall hangings and a few cracked and chipped pieces of pottery, but he couldn't find the papers or the jewel he was looking for. In fact, for an attic that was used to store extra pieces of furniture and items of clothing, it was quite empty. This was another example of how lacking in funds the orphanage was and how desperately they needed the basic supplies to feed and clothe the children.

When Theo finished his search, he extinguished his lantern and left the attic. He reminded himself to speak with Livie about the state of the finances of the orphanage, and what she planned to do to supplement their income. It was obvious something had to be done.

He also reminded himself to begin work on the broken pieces of furniture. At least he could provide the babes with solid cradles in which to sleep. And the rest of the children a place to keep their possessions. He hated to think of them going without even the basics.

The next time he saw Quinn and Jack, he'd ask them if they

had any ideas of how to raise money for the orphanage. Surely they would have some suggestions. Maybe Quinn could even be counted on to make a donation. Or consider sponsoring one of the older children when they were of an age to find employment.

As Theo retraced his way down the stairs, he felt a small bit better. Even though he hadn't found the papers or the jewel, he'd come up with a couple of ideas that would help Livie and the children.

That should ease her mind at least a little. It was obvious how much she worried about the children. Anything he could do for her would help. He owed her that much.

And more.

❦

CHAPTER FOUR

L IVIE STOOD AT her office window and watched as Theo tackled one task after another.

He'd chopped enough wood that they'd have no trouble keeping the rooms toasty warm for at least a week, if not longer. He'd spent several hours in the stable, fixing the roof and caring for the two horses the orphanage kept for emergency use only and weekly trips to the village to pick up supplies.

He'd mucked out the stalls and put fresh hay down. The stable looked clean enough for him to make a room for himself there. Maybe that was his intent. It was a fact he didn't sleep an entire night in the room they'd provided for him.

On the nights Livie spent at the orphanage, she'd seen and heard him roaming about on the ground floor. It was as if he was searching for something, but he wouldn't find anything here. There was nothing to find. The only item she had of any worth was the stone the dying man had given her to give to a man called Jason.

She only wished Jason would arrive and she could give the items to him.

Livie returned to her desk and opened her ledgers to work on the accounts. This wasn't something she looked forward to doing. There was never enough money to go around, but keeping track of how much money they had was something that had to be done.

Livie concentrated on her ledgers until she heard a knock on the door. "What is it, Marie?"

"It's not Marie, Mrs. Matthews. It's me, Theo."

She didn't want his presence to affect her like it did, but without willing it to, her heart skipped a beat, then thundered more rapidly in her breast. "Yes, Captain. Was there something you needed?"

"I'd like to talk to you, if you don't mind."

"Of course," Livie answered. "Please, have a seat."

Theo entered the room and sat in the chair in front of her desk. "I see you're working on your ledgers again. You seem to spend a great deal of time on them."

"It's a necessary part of the job of running the orphanage."

"I imagine it takes a great deal of money to keep so many children fed and clothed day in and day out."

"Yes, it does. It seems like there are more and more children who need us, and less and less money that people have to donate to us."

"I may have a solution to help with that problem, Livie."

Livie felt a glimmer of hope lighten the weight that sat on her chest. "You do?"

"Yes. I have some friends that I served with in the army who have the means to help the children. They could possibly set up a fund in London to donate to The Angel's Wings Orphanage, or sponsor some of the older children when they reach the age to find employment."

Livie couldn't stop her heart from leaping in her breast. "Oh, Theo. That would be wonderful! Even the smallest amount would be welcome, and I've run out of families in the area that I can ask to take in another child."

"Let me write a few letters and I'll see what I can do."

"Oh, Theo, I can't believe this might be possible. Thank you."

"I make no promises, I simply want you to know that I'll do whatever I can."

"I can't ask for anything more."

"I also have another idea."

"What?" she asked. She felt more hopeful than she had for ages.

"I helped Frank cut back the raspberry, blackberry, and gooseberry bushes yesterday. Frank mentioned that the berry bushes were so plentiful that even the orphanage can't begin to use all the fruit they provided."

"That's right. Mrs. Barnes makes more jams than we can use."

"Then, perhaps we could sell them."

"What?"

"Perhaps the children could pick the berries when they are ready, and Mrs. Barnes can organize a day when several of the ladies from the village can come together to make jams and jellies. Then, Frank can take them to London and sell them at the market. Or even perhaps at the hotels and inns in London."

Livie sat behind her desk in stunned amazement. Why had she never thought of this? "That is a wonderful idea, Theo. Absolutely wonderful. Thank you."

"I know how desperately the orphanage needs money. The money from the sale of jars of jams would help."

"Oh, yes it would. It certainly would," Livie said.

"And, I have another question I'd like to ask."

"What is it?"

"I noticed one of the cats living in the stable had a litter of kittens. There looks to be six of them and they have their eyes open now and seem to be quite tame. I thought maybe the children might like to see them."

Livie couldn't keep a smile from brightening her face. "They would love to see them, Captain. Did you want to take them out now?"

"Yes. Before it gets dark."

"I'll have the staff get their coats and gloves on and you can take them to the stable."

Livie rose from her chair and instructed Marie to have the staff put coats, hats, and gloves on the older children and bring them down. When she returned, she found Theo standing before the fire. He turned when she entered.

"How old are the oldest children?" he asked.

"Eight. There are six children between the ages of five and eight."

"Only six?"

"We are mainly a foundling home, Theo. We make every effort to find homes for the children as soon as we can. Those we can't place are moved to St. Joseph's Orphanage in the village when they turn nine."

"What happens to them then?"

"They are educated. They learn to read, write, do their sums, and they are trained in a trade. When they are ready, they are found positions in the better homes in London. They are supervised to make sure they are well trained and that their employers are pleased with them."

"That's quite impressive, Mrs. Matthews."

"We're the only family any of them have. We have an obligation to watch over them until they can fend for themselves."

Livie stood rooted as Theo stepped closer.

"What brought you here, Livie?"

Livie locked her gaze with Theo's and started the well-rehearsed story she'd practiced for when he asked that question, for she knew he would. And she knew she had to be prepared with an answer.

"I wanted to leave London and be on my own. I answered an advertisement in the papers to work here and help the women birth their babes, then to take care of those babies until they were old enough to be on their own. I thought that might be something I could manage, so I took the position. After I was here a while, the supervisory position became available, and I was fortunate to be given it. I have been here ever since."

"Why did you leave your home, Livie? Why didn't you let

your father help you make a match and marry? I know that's what you always wanted."

Livie felt her face grow hot. "That's none of your concern, Theo. In fact, nothing of my personal life is any of your concern."

"I'd like to make it my concern. I feel as if I owe you for the past we shared."

"You owe me nothing except to leave me alone."

Theo's head snapped as if she'd slapped him. "You are right, Mrs. Matthews. Please, forgive me."

Thankfully, the excited voices of the children echoed outside Livie's door and there wasn't another chance for Theo to ask any more questions. Which meant there was no need for Livie to lie any more than she already had.

She opened the door and stood so he could leave. "The children are ready," she said, urging Theo to exit the room.

"Aren't you coming with us?"

"No. I have too much to do here."

"Very well. Perhaps you can have the staff bundle the younger children next. I can take them out when I return with the older children."

Livie nodded, then closed the door behind Theo when he left. She sat down behind her desk and pretended to work on her ledgers again, but she could get no work done. Not when she had other problems to worry about.

She should have refused to let the younger children go to see the kittens. The risk was too great. She doubted he would recognize any of the children, and refusing to allow the younger children to go with him would have drawn more attention than allowing them to go.

But if he did feel a connection to any of the children, the consequences would be tragic.

THEO RETURNED WITH the older children and took the younger children to play with the kittens. Livie paced from one side of her office to the other. On each pass, she stopped to look out the window. What was taking so long? Theo should have had the children back a long time ago. How long did it take for six children to hold kittens? Surely not this long.

She paced the room once more, then stopped at the window again. Theo was leading the children from the barn and bringing them back to the orphanage. The children crowded around him as if he were their hero and they were his loyal servants.

There were smiles on their faces and a bounce to their steps, the same as if they were coming home from a fair. Livie's heart warmed in her breast the closer they came to the house. For the first time, she realized how tall Theo was in comparison to the small three- and four-year-olds. He held two of the children's hands in his and appeared like a giant next to the small children.

Livie's gaze didn't simply focus on the group of six children as a whole, but on one child in particular. Her child. Theo's child.

A lump formed in her throat. The resemblance was remarkable. Livie had never realized it before, but her son had several distinguishing features that were identical to his father's.

Jamie was already taller than any of the children his age and his hair was the exact color of his father's. Even his eyes matched the startling blue of Theo's eyes.

Livie wondered at the fact that Theo didn't see the similarities and realize that Jamie was his. But thankfully, he didn't. And he never would. He could never find out that he had a son, or he'd move heaven and earth to become a part of his son's life. And Livie couldn't allow that. It was one thing to risk Theo being here for a few weeks, or even a month or two. It would be a completely different problem if he discovered he had a son. He wouldn't want to leave him. He might even choose to stay here permanently. She couldn't allow that to happen.

Theo hadn't cared enough to find out if there had been consequences from their nights together. He hadn't wanted her then, and she couldn't allow him to play a part in her life now.

She returned to her desk and pretended interest in the numbers before her. She looked up when there was a knock on the door, but before she could answer, the door opened and Theo stood there with a grin on his face that lit up the entire room.

"You should have seen them, Livie," he said entering the room. "I didn't think I'd be able to get all of the little ones back inside without at least two or three kittens coming along with them."

Livie looked at the twinkle in Theo's eyes. The smile on his face. The two creases on either side of his mouth that dented in deeper when he broadened his smile. The sharp angles of his high cheekbones and rigid jaw. And the white teeth that glimmered when he smiled.

Her heart ached when she looked at him. No person had a right to be this handsome. No man should have the ability to affect her like he did. He was about as perfect as a man could be. And she was as defenseless against him as she'd been five years ago.

"I wish you would have been there, Livie. There was a little girl, I think she must have been the youngest of all of them."

"That would be Mary," Livie said.

"Well, she hid one of the kittens in her pocket. I think she intended to sneak the kitten back with her. If the kitten wouldn't have let out a loud meow, she'd have gotten away with it."

Livie couldn't help but laugh.

"And there was a little boy. He couldn't have been more than four. You should have seen him. He's a born leader. He organized the kittens and gave one to each of the children. He told them they should each choose a name for their kitten. And they did. It was remarkable how he took command of the rest of the children."

Livie didn't volunteer Jamie's name, but she knew that was who Theo was talking about. His leadership quality was a trait he inherited from his father.

"Thank you for doing this for the children, Theo. You gave them a good memory to cherish. They don't have enough of those."

Theo watched her for several moments as if he had the power to see through her and understand all of the emotions she'd kept locked away since he'd walked away from her.

There was something in his gaze that hinted at a regret he felt for leaving her. As if he might do something differently if he had the chance to do that night over again.

But it was too late now. More than four years too late.

Livie turned away from Theo and sat behind her desk.

"Can we start over, Livie?" he asked. "Can we see if our being together might work?"

"It's too late, Theo. More than four years too late."

There was a long pause before he spoke. "If I could, I'd do things differently, Livie."

Livie looked up and stared at him. She forced herself to see past the parts of him she'd fallen in love with. She forced herself to ignore the reasons she still loved him. She couldn't allow them to influence her life, or her decisions, or her heart.

"It's too late, Theo. Our chance to have a life together is long past."

"I was afraid you'd feel that way." He breathed a heavy sigh and watched her for several heart-wrenching moments. "I should get back to work," he said. A knock on the door stopped him.

The door opened and Marie entered. "This came for you, Mrs. Matthews." Marie handed Livie a letter. "They said it was urgent."

Livie opened the missive.

"Is something wrong, Livie?"

"No, nothing's wrong." She lifted her head and locked her gaze with his. "Captain Dunworthy, would you see that the horses are hitched to the wagon first thing in the morning?" she said before Theo left the room.

"Yes, Mrs. Matthews. Of course."

"I just have to go to the village in the morning. And, Marie. Get a room ready. I'll be bringing back another young lady."

"Very well, Mrs. Matthews," Marie answered, then left the room.

When Livie looked up, Theo was still in the room staring at her. "Are you sure everything's all right, Livie?"

"Yes, Captain. Everything's fine."

Theo watched her for a moment, then turned to leave.

"Theo?" Livie said before Theo reached the door.

"Yes."

"I hate to ask you this, but would you mind driving me to the village in the morning?"

"Of course not."

Theo gave her a confused look, then turned. "I'll see you in the morning, then."

"Yes. In the morning. And Theo?" she said before he was gone.

"Yes, ma'am."

"Do you have a weapon?"

Theo's eyebrows shot upward. "Yes. A pistol."

"Would you please bring it with you?"

"Livie?" he asked. A frown deepened across his forehead. "What is—?"

"That's all, Theo," Livie answered, putting an end to his question.

"Yes, ma'am," he said, then he left.

CHAPTER FIVE

THEO ROSE EARLY the next morning and hitched the horses to the wagon, then waited for Livie to join him. Before she arrived, Frank came with several quilts and pillows. Something wasn't right, but Theo didn't know what it was.

It wasn't long before Livie arrived with several pastries wrapped in a linen cloth and a flask of hot coffee. Theo helped her atop the wagon, and they took off.

Without speaking, she handed him a pastry, then held the jar of coffee for him. They ate and drank in silence. Having a conversation was something they previously had never had trouble with, but this morning, Livie looked too worried and preoccupied to find words to speak.

"Very well," Theo said when they'd finished their coffee and pastry. "When are you going to tell me what's wrong?"

Livie folded her hands in her lap and clutched her fingers in a tight grip. "It's the young lady we're going to get to take back with us."

"What about her?"

"She's in danger and we need to get her to The Angel's Wings as quickly as possible."

"What is she in danger from?"

"She shouldn't be traveling."

"Why not?"

"Her baby is due any moment now. It's not safe for her to travel this close to when her baby might arrive, but..." She paused. "But in this case, it is unavoidable."

"Why is it unavoidable?"

"Because the father of the babe is the Duke of Westling's son, the Earl of Hollingsdale."

"Westling? Why does that name sound familiar?"

Theo tried to remember what he'd heard about the Duke of Westling's son, but couldn't.

"It sounds familiar because His Grace's son was involved in a scandal a few months ago."

"That's right. I remember now. He was killed in a duel."

"Yes. The Earl of Cashton challenged Westling's son when he got his sister pregnant and refused to marry her."

"Quite noble of him."

"That's no doubt what Cashton thought, which was no doubt why he challenged the duke's son to a duel."

"But why are we going to get Cashton's sister?"

"The Earl of Hollingsdale was Westling's only heir. With Hollingsdale dead, the Westling line will cease to exist. I believe the Duke of Westling is in hopes that Cashton's sister will give birth to a son, a son he can petition the Queen to name his legitimate heir."

"Can the Queen do that?"

"It's not common, but yes, she can, since there is no heir to the dukedom. Rumor has it that the Queen owes Westling a great deal of money and Westling has agreed to forgive the debt if the Queen will grant him an heir."

"So, what is Cashton's sister doing here?"

"When the Lady Dianna refused to live under the Duke of Westling's roof and be a part of his family until the child was born, Westling attempted to kidnap her. To avoid being held captive by the Duke of Westling, Lady Dianna ran away. Somehow, she found her way here and is seeking sanctuary at The Angel's Wings."

"And you intend to take her in?"

"I can't refuse her. She's in danger."

"Livie, do you realize the danger you are in by taking her in?"

"I don't have a choice, Theo. I can't turn her away."

"If there's a chance she could provide the Duke of Westling with an heir, His Grace isn't going to let the lady get away from him until he knows if the babe she delivers is a boy or a girl."

"I know," Livie whispered.

At least Livie knew the danger she was in, especially if she planned to go through with it.

Theo looked at the open road on which they traveled. He didn't like the idea of traveling out in the open once they got the Lady Dianna and made their way back to The Angel's Wings. If Westling knew where they were, there was no way Theo could protect the lady or Livie.

"Where are we going to meet this young lady?"

"At the church. She is staying with the vicar and his wife."

"You'll have to give me directions."

Livie nodded, then led him to the vicar's house.

"I'll go in and get her," Livie said when they arrived in front of the parsonage.

"Be careful."

"There's nothing to fear. I doubt His Grace knows Lady Dianna is even here yet."

Theo hoped Livie was right. He didn't relish the thought that he'd be forced to use the pistol he'd brought.

Livie knocked on the vicar's door and entered the small house. A few minutes later, she returned with a young lady that looked as frightened as anyone he'd ever seen. He helped Livie and the Lady Dianna into the back of the wagon and got them settled.

"Theo?" Livie said before he stepped atop the wagon. "Go as fast as you can. I don't want this babe to come before we reach The Angel's Wings."

Theo locked his gaze with Livie's and saw the seriousness in her eyes.

Theo didn't want the babe to come out in the open where the Duke of Westling could come upon them without warning either, but from the look of the Lady Dianna, they might not have a choice. Every indication was that she was ready to have her baby right now.

⇛⇚

LIVIE KNEW THEO drove the team of horses as fast as possible without hitting every rut and pothole in the road, but it still seemed as if it took forever to reach The Angel's Wings. Lady Dianna's birthing pains had started almost as soon as they'd left the vicar's cottage, and they'd worsened with each clop of the horses' hooves. She was struggling to be brave, but her moans gradually grew louder and now were cries of agony.

"Do you want me to pull to the side of the road, Livie?"

Livie locked her gaze with Lady Dianna's and the brave lady shook her head.

"We can't stop," Lady Dianna gasped. "I can't be found in the open."

"Very well," Livie said, then turned to Theo. "Go on, Theo."

He gave her a nod of agreement, then pushed the team to go faster.

Livie had never considered the distance from the orphanage to the vicar's cottage that far, but today it seemed different. Today Livie didn't think they'd ever reach The Angel's Wings, but finally the stone building came within view.

Theo turned into the lane and made his way to the front of the orphanage. The minute he stopped the team of horses, he jumped down and ran to the back.

As if she weighed nothing, he picked Lady Dianna up and carried her into the building.

"This way," Livie said and led him up the stairs and to the

room where Marie stood at the door.

"I'll stand watch," he said when he'd placed her on the bed.

Livie nodded and concentrated on taking care of Lady Dianna.

She was young and frightened, and Livie could tell the birth wasn't going to be easy. The babe wasn't small and was turned the wrong way for an easy birth. Livie reached for her hand and tried to give her the courage she'd need to have this baby. But there was so much working against the young girl.

Hour after hour the young lady struggled to birth her babe and Livie knew if the babe didn't come soon, Lady Dianna would grow too weak to bring her infant into the world.

"Go below and get some fresh cloths," Marie said issuing a command. "You need to leave the room for a moment."

Livie didn't want to leave the girl, but Lady Dianna's struggle was wearing her down. "I'll be right back, Marie."

"Yes. You just need to be gone for a moment or two."

Livie nodded, then rushed from the room. The moment she stepped into the hall, the world came crashing down around her. The weight of Lady Dianna's struggle was almost too much for her to bear.

What if the young girl lost the babe? What if she was not strong enough to survive such a difficult birth? What if she died?

Livie clutched her stomach and doubled over in pain. Before she could recover, Theo's strong arms wrapped around her and gathered her to him.

He wrapped his arms around her and nestled her close to him.

"She'll come through this, Livie. With your help, she'll be fine."

Before she could stop them, the tears she'd held at bay rushed forward. Violent sobs shook her body and her knees threatened to give out from beneath her.

"Shh, sweetheart," Theo said, rubbing his hand up and down her spine. "Everything will be fine."

"Oh, Theo. She's so fragile. And she's growing weaker by the minute."

"Tell her not to give up. Tell her that her child needs her. That she has to live for the sake of the baby."

Livie looked up and her gaze locked with Theo's. Those words were the same that she'd been told when birthing Jamie and she'd wanted to give up – that she had to live for the sake of her child, that if she gave up, her child would have no one to love him.

Livie took a deep breath and stepped away from Theo. She turned, then opened the door.

The Lady Dianna needed to know how desperately her child needed her. The lady needed to realize that if she weren't there to take care of her child, there was no one who would. Unless the child was a boy. Then, the Duke of Westling would steal him away from her and raise him as his own.

Livie paused a moment then stepped inside. She was met by a pitiful moan.

"The child is coming, my lady," Marie said, clutching the lady's hand. "Push, my lady."

"I can't," were the only words Lady Dianna said.

"You must," Livie answered her. "Your child needs you. He will not survive without you."

The weak and exhausted lady opened her eyes enough to lock with Livie's. "Promise me that you… won't let my baby die. Please." The young girl gasped through the pain.

"Your baby won't die, my lady. I promise."

"I want… you… to keep her. She's… yours."

"Don't say that, my lady. You'll be here to take care of her. You'll be here to watch her grow."

"No," the lady moaned as she was attacked by another stabbing pain.

"Your babe is coming," Marie said excitedly.

"Push, Lady Dianna. Once more," Livie encouraged. "Push."

And Lady Dianna struggled one last time. Thankfully, the

baby entered the world with a strong, healthy cry.

"Your child is here, my lady. It's a little girl. A healthy little girl."

Lady Dianna opened her eyes long enough to lock her gaze with Livie's. It was almost as if it was a plea for Livie to take care of her infant, and be the mama Lady Dianna would never be to her daughter.

Before Livie could encourage the young mother to fight to stay alive, Lady Dianna closed her eyes in peaceful rest.

"Dianna!" Livie yelled and grabbed the young girl's shoulders. "Look at me! Don't leave me! Don't leave your daughter!"

But it was too late. The young lady was gone and refused to come back.

CHAPTER SIX

LIVIE SAT AT the bedside for a very long time. She couldn't bring herself to leave Lady Dianna. She was so young, with so much of her life left to live. And that life had been cut short. She'd left her innocent babe without a mother.

Tears she couldn't keep from spilling over her lashes ran down her cheeks, and harsh, painful sobs tore at her insides. No matter what she did, she couldn't stop the ache from consuming her.

No matter what she'd done or said, she hadn't been able to stop the young lady from giving up.

Livie held Lady Dianna's hand and rubbed gentle circles against her flesh. Life had been so unfair to her. And to her babe.

Finally, the tears stopped running down her cheeks and the wracking sobs that she couldn't keep at bay ceased. There was nothing she could do to stop the thudding in her head. Every inch of her ached with a pain that would not ease. If only things had not turned out the way they had. If only the man who'd got her with child would have married her.

If only the man who'd got Livie with child had married *her*.

"Mrs. Matthews?" Marie said from beside her.

Livie lifted her gaze and wiped the tears with a cloth she had in her hands. "Yes, Marie."

"Can I get you anything?"

"No, I'm fine. How is the babe?"

"She's a fine, healthy lass. One of Frank's daughters is here to feed her. You might want to go below, however, and talk to Captain Dunworthy. He thinks he sees activity outside. He's concerned it might be the duke."

Livie made her way out of the room and down the stairs. When she reached the foyer, Theo stood watch at the window.

"Is someone here?"

"Yes. They're at the end of the lane."

"Do you think it's the Duke of Westling?"

"It could be." He stopped talking and looked at her. Livie knew her eyes were red and swollen. She knew he couldn't miss the fact that she'd been crying.

Thankfully, he didn't ask her about Lady Dianna. Instead, he gathered her in his arms and held her close. He nestled her against him and rubbed her arms and her back, then he tilted her head upward and kissed her cheek. Then her forehead.

"Oh, Livie. My sweet, sweet Livie."

Livie's voice trembled when she spoke. "I couldn't save her."

Theo shook his head. "It wasn't meant to be. God wanted her to live with Him. That's what I had to tell myself whenever I lost one of the men in my command. God wanted them with Him more than here."

"How did you do it? I only see someone die every once in a while. You watched young men die every day after every battle. How did you handle it?"

"I'm not sure I ever did." Theo brought her in closer and held her tight. "I still see their faces at night when I close my eyes. I still hear their cries of pain when the air is still. I think I always will."

"Oh, Theo," Livie said, holding him and comforting him. He needed her as much as she needed him.

Theo held her with a strength she needed more than anything else. He'd always been the strength she needed – until he wasn't there when she needed him most. If only she could go back to that time in her life and change what had happened. But it was useless to wish for things to be different when it was impossible to change them.

The house was quiet except for the usual muffled sounds of children's laughter and the staff walking from place to place.

Theo finally broke the silence. "What did the Lady Dianna have? Was it a boy or a girl?"

"A girl. A sweet baby girl."

"What are you going to do?"

"I don't know. It depends on what His Grace plans to do."

"We'll find out soon enough," Theo said, looking out the window. "His Grace is here."

Livie looked out the window and saw an elderly, gray-haired man dismounting his horse and coming to the door. He walked with a small army of men to do his bidding.

The knock on the door was solid, leaving no mistake as to its demand to be admitted. Livie answered the knock.

"Welcome, Your Grace," she said, stepping back to allow him to enter.

Without a word of greeting, the Duke of Westling entered the foyer like an angry thundercloud.

"Where is she?"

"By *she*, I assume you mean Lady Dianna."

"You know damn good and well that's who I mean."

"Watch how you talk to the lady, Your Grace," Theo said taking a step forward.

"And who do you think you are to give me orders?"

"I'm the man who is going to kick your arse out of that door if you don't show the lady the respect she deserves."

"Fool! Don't you see the army of men standing behind me?"

"Oh, I see them," Theo said, as he removed the gun from beneath his jacket and pointed it at the Duke of Westling's heart. "But you'll be dead long before they can step through the door to save you."

Livie's breath caught in her throat. This was a side of Theo she hadn't previously seen. A side of him that was an example of the fierce soldier he was reputed to be. The brave, and even reckless officer that he had been, who would face some of the highest ranking nobility of the *ton* regardless of the consequences.

Livie watched as the Duke of Westling considered his reaction to Theo's threat and she knew the confrontation could go either way.

Eventually, the bluster left the duke and his shoulders sagged. "Excuse me, ma'am," he said in a more conciliatory tone. "I've come to ask about Lady Dianna. I was told she was here."

"Yes, Your Grace. She is. But… Could we speak privately?"

"That's not necessary."

"I'm afraid it is."

Livie didn't know if the tone of her voice alerted him that something was wrong, or if the look on her face and the tears that sprang in her eyes were the reason, but the Duke of Westling became more obliging.

"Very well."

Livie led him to her office and showed him to a seat. Once there, she poured a glass of brandy and handed it to him. "You perhaps will need this."

"The news you have is bad," he said as a statement.

"Yes, Your Grace. It is. I'm afraid the young lady you seek died a few hours ago giving birth to your grandchild."

"My grandchild?"

"Yes, Your Grace."

"Was the child a boy?"

"Does that matter?"

"Of course it does," he said in a gruff voice.

"No, Your Grace. The child was not a boy. It was a beautiful, healthy baby girl. Would you like to see her?"

The Duke of Westling was devastated by the news. All color left his face and his hands fisted at his sides. An agonizing moan escaped into the room that turned into a growl of despair.

"I'm sorry, Your Grace. Would you like to see your granddaughter?"

"No, I do not want to see her. She is the reason my son is dead. It is because of her that the Westling dukedom will cease to exist."

His gaze shot upward and locked with Livie's. There was nothing in his expression but bitterness and hatred.

"No! I do not want to see her!" he said again. "I do not ever want to lay eyes on her or I might do her harm."

"The child is but hours old, Your Grace. She's the innocent party in this tragedy."

"She is the *cause* of this tragedy!"

"Can't you find it in your heart to take responsibility for the child? She is of your blood."

"No! She is a bastard. She is the reason my son is dead. I want nothing to do with her. Not now. Not ever!"

"She is your son's child."

"She is nothing to me. Nothing, do you hear me?" With those words the Duke of Westling rose on legs that threatened to collapse beneath him and walked from the room.

Theo left with the duke.

When she was alone, the room spun around her and there was a terrible ringing in her ears.

Livie struggled to catch her breath and she reached out to steady herself, but there was nothing there for her to hold on to. Before she could catch herself, the room went dark and the floor came up to meet her.

THEO WATCHED FROM the front until he was sure Westling was gone, then turned to return to Livie. He knew how upset she was, knew how Westling's words had bothered her. How could they not? She'd just watched a young lady die while birthing her babe. Then listened while the grandfather of that innocent babe had threatened to do it harm.

He walked into Livie's office and did not see her at first. At second glance, he saw her crumpled form on the floor.

"Livie!"

Theo rushed to her side and lifted her into his arms. "Livie? Livie?" He carried her to the sofa and placed her on the cushions. "Look at me, Livie."

He touched her cheek and brushed his fingers across her brow. Her flesh was cold and clammy. He pressed his finger against her wrist. Her pulse was slow and unsteady.

"Marie!"

It didn't take Livie's assistant long to arrive.

"What happened?" she asked, racing into the room.

"She lost consciousness."

"This day has been too much for her. She's had too much to contend with the past few weeks."

Theo didn't know what Marie meant, but he swore he would find out. He couldn't let Livie work herself like she had. The mental and physical stress had taken its toll.

"Marie, get some water. And have Mrs. Barnes prepare a tea tray." He looked at Marie before she left. "When's the last time she ate?"

"I don't know, Captain. Not today, I know. Or maybe even yesterday."

"Tell Mrs. Barnes to send something for her to eat."

"Yes. Right away, Captain."

"Livie? Livie, please. Wake up." Theo knelt beside the sofa and held Livie's hand. He was frightened by how lifeless she seemed. She should have awakened by now.

"Here," Marie said, handing him a cool, wet cloth.

Theo placed the cloth on Livie's face and at first there was no reaction. Slowly, she turned her head a little, then more.

"Livie?"

"Mmm," she groaned.

"Wake up, Livie. Here. Drink this." He placed a glass of water to her lips and forced her to drink.

"Do you have some wine?" he asked Marie.

"Yes, in the kitchen."

"Get it."

Marie raced from the room again and returned a moment later with a half-full bottle of wine. Theo poured a small amount in a glass and held it to Livie's lips.

She took one swallow then sputtered and sat up to catch her breath.

"That's better," Theo said in relief. "You've slept long enough."

"What happened?"

"You lost consciousness."

"Is Westling gone?"

"Yes. You don't have to worry about him anymore."

Marie entered the room with a tray of tea and some sandwiches. "Welcome back, Mrs. Matthews. You gave us quite a scare."

"I didn't mean to, Marie. I don't know what happened."

"You've gone too long without enough rest and nothing to eat. And the last few days haven't exactly been easy."

"No," Livie answered. "How is the babe?"

"She's fine. She's a strong, healthy one."

"Have you notified Lady Dianna's family?"

"Yes," Marie answered. "I wrote them and Frank took the message to the village to send it. They should get it in a day or two."

"Good. Let me know what they decide as soon as you hear."

"Very good. Now, I'll leave you alone so you can eat. Mrs. Barnes says she doesn't want any of her sandwiches to come back uneaten."

"Thank Mrs. Barnes, and tell her I'll try. Perhaps Captain Dunworthy can help me."

"All I'll do to help you is hand you the next sandwich and make sure you eat it."

Marie smiled and left the room, closing the door behind her.

"Eat," Theo said, handing Livie a small sandwich.

"I can't eat all of these," Livie said between bites.

"I know," Theo said, watching her eat. "Just eat what you can. You must be starved."

"I am," she answered. "I didn't realize how hungry I was."

"How do you feel?"

"I've felt better."

"I don't doubt it, Livie. But at least a little of your color has returned."

Theo reached for another sandwich and watched while Livie ate it. When he tried to give her another one, she held up her hand and refused it.

"No more. Please."

"If you say so," he said on a laugh. "You did an admirable job. Mrs. Barnes should be pleased."

Livie smiled and Theo couldn't stop a smile from lifting the corners of his mouth.

"Thank you, Theo," she said, looking at him. "I don't know what I would have done without you here with me. I don't even want to think of having to face Westling on my own."

"I don't either. It's hard to say what he would have done if you would have been alone. He's the type of man who is used to getting what he wants."

"I know," she answered.

Her gaze locked with his and held it. An unfamiliar rush of something warmed his heart. He stared at her, then slowly lowered his head and pressed his lips to hers.

He hadn't intended to give in to the emotions he felt, but couldn't help himself. He'd been drawn to her when he'd first met her more than four years ago, but hadn't been disciplined enough to keep himself from taking her, even though he knew their feelings couldn't go anywhere. He needed to escape the plans his father had concocted for him.

His father was convinced Theo should become a vicar. That

Theo should live the life of a clergyman. Yet, Theo knew he would wither and die if he was confined to a pulpit. He always knew that he wanted to go into the military. He needed a life of adventure and taking risks. Not the sedate life of comforting and consoling.

And not once did he regret the path he'd chosen, except for two things. That he was abroad when his father died. That he hadn't been home to mend the rift that separated him from his father. That he hadn't been at his father's bedside to tell him that he loved him one last time before he died. And…

That he'd abandoned Livie without telling her goodbye.

He would always regret those two things. But maybe this time he would have the opportunity to tell her that he wouldn't ever leave her again without telling her goodbye.

Or maybe he would never leave her.

Ever.

✦

CHAPTER SEVEN

L IVIE KNEW SHE shouldn't let Theo kiss her. She knew she should stop him from igniting the fire that burned deep inside her, but she couldn't. She needed him too much. She needed his touch, his caress, and his kisses.

Nothing drove her to the brink of madness as much as his lips pressed to hers. Or his muscled back and arms beneath her palms. Or the heat from his body warming her. Or the fire from his kisses causing her to go up in flames. No matter how desperate she was to stop him, she didn't have the willpower to do it.

The emotion his kisses exposed had been evident from the first time he'd kissed her. He wasn't the first man she'd kissed – yet he was. No kiss she'd received was as powerful as his. The moment his lips touched hers, she felt as if she'd never been kissed before, and she never wanted to be kissed by anyone other than Theo ever again.

He deepened his kisses. He demanded more of her and she couldn't deny him.

She relived their nights of unbridled passion and remembered the magic that sparked between them when they touched each other, when their bodies connected, and she knew she could never have enough of that passion. The nights when they'd lain with each other played in her mind and she couldn't stop the memories from consuming her thoughts. No matter what she did, she could never keep the times she'd given herself to Theo from appearing even when she bid them not to.

Then, without allowing them to, fear and panic rose deep inside her, the same as it had when she realized she was with child and Theo had abandoned her. The anger she heard in her father's voice and the disappointment she saw on her mama's face when it became obvious that she was with child flashed in her mind. And the terror that had consumed her when she was forced to leave her home and her family was a bitter memory she could never forget. The helplessness she felt as a single woman with no place to go, and no one to help her returned to haunt her. Not even Theo was there to protect her. The one person who should have been her rock and support had abandoned her without saying goodbye.

Livie unwrapped her arms from around Theo's neck and turned her head to break off their kiss.

"We can't, Theo. You promised you wouldn't."

Livie stepped away from him and turned her back to him.

"Livie, I—"

"You need to leave."

"No, Livie. You need me and I need you."

"You're five years too late, Theo. I needed you five years ago, but I don't need you now. I've learned to survive on my own. I no longer need to rely on you only to have you abandon me again. Those days are over. Please, leave."

"Very well," he said taking one step to the door. "I have work to do."

"No, Theo. I want you to leave The Angel's Wings and never come back."

Livie turned her head. She had to break her contact with Theo. She couldn't stand to look at the disbelief and disappointment on his face.

"You can't mean that. You need me here, Livie, and I need to be here."

"I can't afford for you to be here. I'm not safe when you're here. You cause me nothing but pain and heartache. I can't let you hurt me any longer. I can't."

The silence that engulfed the room was deafening. The cavernous void that silence implied left a gaping hole in her chest. And yet, there was Jamie to think about. She'd been lucky so far that Theo hadn't recognized the similarities between him and his son.

"There's still work to be done here," he answered her. "There's more I need to do."

"What just happened proves that you can't stay. I can't go through losing you again, Theo. I can't."

"What do you mean you can't go through losing me again?"

"Just what I said. A part of me died when you left me five years ago. A part of me that has never recovered."

"Don't do this, Livie. Don't send me away. You need me. Now more than ever."

"I don't need you. I can't risk keeping you with me. What just happened proved that."

"It won't happen again, Livie. I promise."

"You can't make such a promise. You won't keep it."

"Just give me another chance. Let me stay a little while longer."

Livie turned her back to him and braced her hands on the top of the desk. "I need to be alone, Theo. I need to think. Go help Frank. Now."

Livie hung her head between her outstretched arms and squeezed her eyes shut. Finally, she heard the door close softly behind him and knew she was alone. She was unable to focus on anything as the first tear ran down her cheek.

She should hate him. Instead, she loved him more than she had the day she'd met him. More than she'd loved him five years ago when she'd given him her body and he'd stolen her heart.

HE COULDN'T LEAVE her. He knew that now. Not only did she possess the papers and the jewel, and he couldn't leave without them. But he loved her too much to ever abandon her again. He'd left her once. He refused to leave her again. She deserved more. She deserved to be loved.

Theo walked to the barn and fed and watered the horses. He worked tirelessly for hours without slowing down even once. He had too much to consider. Too much to sort out in his mind. Why hadn't Wallace arrived with the message? It had been long enough. He should have been here weeks ago. Unless something had happened to him.

Theo continued with his work until he heard a rustling noise in the back of the barn. He put down his pitchfork and slowly made his way to the back.

"About time you showed up," Jack's voice whispered from a corner in the back stall.

Theo stared at his fellow agent and breathed a sigh of relief. "Did you miss me?"

"I've missed you. Quinn has missed you. And the Home Office has missed you. They want to know what is taking you so bloody long."

"I haven't found anything yet. I'm not sure the papers and jewel are even here."

"What do you mean you're not sure they're here? They have to be here. Wallace left France with them weeks ago."

"How do you know that?"

"Waterford got a message saying so. They want to know why we haven't sent a reply."

Theo raked his hands through his hair in frustration. "If they're here, I bloody well can't find them. And I've searched every inch of this place."

"What kind of place is this?"

"It's a foundling home for unwed mothers and an orphanage for babes who have no family to take them."

"Bloody Hell," Jack cursed under his breath. "Why did Wallace choose this place to meet?"

"Probably because other than one handyman to do odd chores, what other men would come here? They don't even get visitors here."

"Good point," Jack answered. "Is that your role? Do you help out here?"

"Yes. I do odd jobs. Taking care of the horses, cutting wood, patching roofs and doing whatever needs to be done."

"Are you sure the jewel and papers aren't here?"

"If they are, I haven't found them."

"Look again, Theo. We have to find the papers and that jewel. It's important."

"Do you think I haven't looked for them? I have, but I can't find them."

"We're running out of time."

"What do you mean?"

"The French know we don't have them. They also know Wallace took them and hasn't given them to anyone yet. Intelligence tells us they think he's dead."

"Has his body been recovered?"

"No. Which means he either has the papers and jewel with him, or he gave them to someone after he left France."

"Do they think he gave them to someone here?"

"Yes. We tracked him this far then lost his trail. If he's dead, it's likely someone here has the papers and jewel."

Theo raked his fingers through his hair. Who would Wallace have given them to? Who would he have trusted enough to hand over something that valuable? The only person to come to mind was… Livie.

An icy cold surge of dread flowed through his veins.

Theo imagined what might happen to her if Livie had the papers and the jewel. He imagined the danger she would be in. If Wallace gave them to Livie, she was in grave danger. The French wouldn't give up until they found them. And they wouldn't hesitate to kill Livie to get them. Theo had to find them first. And soon. There was no chance the French would stop looking for them until they knew they were in London and out of their reach.

"I'll go through every room again," Theo told Jack. "If they are here, I'll find them."

Jack nodded in agreement. "One more thing," he said before he left.

"What?

"All indications point to the fact that there's a traitor in the agency. Someone who knows every move we intend to make before we make it. And they're selling that information to the French."

Another wave of cold dread washed through Theo's veins. "Are you sure?"

"Yes. That's why we think Wallace is dead. Someone told the French he was coming after the jewel and the papers. They were waiting for him."

"Do we have any idea who this traitor is?"

"No," Jack said. "Just be careful. Don't trust anyone. I'll be back in a couple of days. Hopefully, you'll have found what you're looking for by then."

Theo checked to make sure the coast was clear, then motioned for Jack to leave. He'd search for the missing jewel and papers again tonight. And he wouldn't give up until he found them.

⟫⟪

FOR THREE NIGHTS, Theo searched every room he could think of to search and still there were no papers or the jewel to be found. Where could they be? Theo weighed all possibilities. The first was that the jewel and the papers weren't here. That Wallace hadn't made it to The Angel's Wings. That someone had gotten to him before he made it this far. That was indeed a possibility.

A second scenario was that he'd made it to The Angel's

Wings and had given what he'd taken out of France to someone and they were hiding it. That was a greater possibility considering Wallace's body hadn't been found anywhere.

What could he have done with them?

Theo went to Livie's office and started another search. This room was the most likely room where they had been hidden if they were here. He started with her desk and opened the top drawer, then worked his way through the rest of the drawers. He was concentrating so intensely he didn't realize someone had entered the room.

"Are you looking for something?"

Theo glanced up and his eyes locked with Livie's. He'd known the chances of being discovered were likely, but it was a risk he'd been forced to take.

"Yes, Livie. Actually, I was."

"And what might that be?"

"Something that has significant value to our government."

Livie's eyes opened wide in astonishment. "Our government?"

"Yes."

"Do you work for the government?"

"Yes."

"Are you a spy?"

"I'm a special agent. I do jobs no one else wants to do."

"I see. Is that why you're here? To find something you think we are hiding?"

"Yes."

She entered the room and closed the door behind her. "I should have known. Being a soldier was always important to you. More important than anything or anyone."

"That's not fair, Livie."

"It's more than fair, Theo. I'm living proof of it."

"Livie—"

"Why would you think whatever you're searching for might be here?"

"Because our intelligence indicates it is."

"And what is this object?"

"Papers and a jewel of some kind that one of our agents took from the French."

"Papers?"

"Yes."

"And these papers are important to the government?"

Theo didn't want to answer that question. He couldn't.

"I see," Livie said in a soft whisper.

"I need those papers, Livie. If you have them, it's important that you hand them over."

"Why?"

"Because they contain information that is vital to our national security."

"What information, Theo?"

"I can't tell you that."

"More secrets," she said on a sigh. "And what were you going to do when you found your papers and the jewel? Leave without saying goodbye? Like you did the last time you abandoned me?"

"That's not fair, Livie."

"Isn't it? That's exactly what you did."

Theo didn't speak for several moments. "I need those papers, Livie," he finally said. "You're not safe if you have them."

"I don't."

Theo sucked in a breath. He was so sure if anyone had the papers and the jewel it was Livie. He was sure Wallace had given them to her.

"Are you sure you don't know where they are?"

Theo waited for what seemed forever. Finally, she spoke. "I don't know anything about any papers. Or the jewel. I don't have either of them."

She was lying.

"We're not the only one who wants those papers, Livie. The French want them, too. If you have them, it's important that you hand them over before someone gets hurt. Before you get hurt.

Or the children."

Livie's gaze snapped to lock with his and her expression turned frightening at the mention of the children. "I told you I don't have them. Now, leave me alone and get out of here."

"Do you think the people who want those papers back are above using the children to get what they want? No, Livie. They'll use anyone who gets in their way. And they want those papers."

"I don't have them!" she yelled.

She was lying. At least Theo thought she was.

There was a time when he knew her so well he would have known if she was lying or not. But that was when he was sure Livie was the woman he loved. The woman he would always love. A woman he was certain would never lie to him. But not anymore. Now, he wasn't sure if she was lying or not. She'd closed herself off to him and wouldn't let him in.

Theo paced the floor, then stopped and raked his fingers through his hair.

"The French won't give up until they have the papers and jewel in their possession. They won't give up until they've done everything in their power to get them back. No matter who gets hurt in the process."

"Get out, Theo. Leave me alone!"

"You're not safe, Livie. And neither are the children."

"Get out, Theo!"

Theo walked toward the door and left. She'd left him no choice. He had to do everything in his power to protect her. And the children.

LIVIE PACED HER bedroom floor, back and forth, then back again. She couldn't come to terms with the lie she'd told Theo. She couldn't believe that it had been impossible to trust him enough to tell him that she had the papers and the jewel. That meant that she thought he might be the traitor. That she could believe that he wasn't trustworthy when she knew he was, even if he'd abandoned her when she'd needed him most.

She thought of the man she'd found in the snow. The man who'd been shot and died in her arms. He'd only asked one thing of her. That she take the papers and the jewel and keep them safe until she could give them to someone named Jason.

The man claimed that someone in the agency was a traitor.

Livie would give anything if she could trust Theo, but she couldn't. She wouldn't allow him to deceive her again. She'd done that once and she'd paid a heavy price.

Livie left her room and made her way to where Jamie slept. She entered his room and knelt at his bedside, then reached for his hand and held it. She needed to be close to him. Holding his hand allowed her to feel closer to Theo. Seeing the precious angel that she and Theo had created made the times they'd spent together magical.

She knew she should feel guilty for giving herself to Theo, but how could she? Not when something so wonderful had come from their time together. She could never regret one moment of the time they'd spent together. Jamie had been created out of the love she and Theo had felt for each other, and when Jamie was older, she'd tell him about his father so that he never forgot him.

Even if Theo hated her when he discovered he had a son that she'd never told him about.

CHAPTER EIGHT

L IVIE COULDN'T REMEMBER the last time she'd got a decent night's sleep. The minute she closed her eyes she relived the night the agent had given her the papers and the jewel he'd taken from the French. And she recalled every word he'd said to her. His plea not to trust anyone except the man called Jason.

Surely she could trust Theo, though. Couldn't she?

But that's what she thought when she'd lain with him, until she realized she was carrying his child and he had left her.

Livie relived those terrifying days as if they had happened yesterday. She relived the anger and the disappointment on her parents' faces when she was forced to admit that she was carrying a child and the father of that child had abandoned her. When her father, the local vicar, had forced her from his home because of her disgrace. When she was forced to find her way to The Angel's Wings to have her baby alone, and all she wanted to do was die.

Livie broke out in a cold sweat and threw the covers from her body. When she couldn't force herself to remain in bed any longer, she rose, dressed, and went to her office. If she couldn't sleep, she could at least get some work done. Marie had made a list of all the clothes the children had outgrown and would need to be replaced when the weather turned warmer.

That also meant additional expenses for the orphanage. In the last two weeks alone, they'd taken in three expectant mothers about to have their babes. This would increase the amount of food they'd need, and they'd have to hire at least one more staff to care for the mothers and their babies. They'd also need at least one more wet nurse, and someone to do the washing. And Mrs. Barnes could use an extra scullery maid to help in the kitchen.

It never ended. The need was always greater than the supply.

Livie worked on her books for what seemed an eternity, then paused when she experienced the feeling that she was being watched. She looked up to find Theo leaning against the open door frame with his arms crossed over his chest and one booted foot crossed atop the opposite foot.

She looked out the window and saw that it was still dark outside. "What time is it?" she asked, looking at the clock on the mantle.

"It's almost four o'clock," he answered, then pushed himself away from the door frame and entered the room.

"What are you doing up already?" she asked.

"I couldn't sleep," he answered.

"It must be a night for staying awake," Livie answered.

"What's keeping you from falling asleep, Livie?"

Livie sat back in her chair and rolled her stiff shoulders.

"Here," Theo said. "It's time you rested for a few minutes. Come sit over here. I'd like to talk to you."

He led her to the sofa before the fire. When she sat, he placed a log in the grate and the fire came to life.

"What would you like to talk about?" she asked, trying to sound as calm as possible.

"Several things, Livie."

"Such as?"

"What was your husband's name, Livie?"

Her heart stuttered in her breast. "Why do you want to know?"

"No reason."

"Then there's no reason to tell you."

"Were you happy?"

"Of course I was. I married him, after all."

"That doesn't mean you were happy."

"Well, I was."

"What did he do?"

"Enough, Theo."

"I just want to know all about you after I left."

"My," Livie said, trying to pretend a lackadaisical attitude. "Such a lot of questions about my personal life. One would almost think you cared."

"I do. I always have."

"No. You were only interested in my body and how you could use me."

"No, Livie. That's not true and you know it."

"No, Theo. You were never interested in me. Especially when I needed you to be, you weren't."

She'd said too much. If she let her emotions run away with her, she'd reveal things she shouldn't, and yet... The way she'd felt the first months after she realized she was carrying Theo's child and she had no one to turn to and no one to comfort her came back to torment her. She'd wanted to lash out at the man who'd abandoned her. She wanted him to suffer the same as she had.

The day when she'd told her parents that she was with child rose from the ashes as if to destroy her, the same as it had when she'd lived through that nightmare the first time.

What had she expected her father to do? He was a vicar. His father was the Earl of Everley. He had a name to uphold. A reputation. He could hardly allow his unmarried daughter to parade into church with her belly huge with child. So, he was forced to do the only thing he could. He banned her from the church. Banned her from his home. Banned her from ever stepping foot near her family ever again. And Livie was forced to set out on her own to find a place that would take her in. Thank Heaven she found The Angel's Wings.

"Is your husband still alive?"

"No, he's dead."

"How did he die?"

"In the war, Theo. You, more than anyone know how many men died in the war."

"Yes. I do. We lost too many men."

Livie didn't want to share more with Theo. She didn't want to make up a fake story about a fake husband and a fake life she'd never lived.

"How are your parents? Are they well?"

"You've asked enough!"

Livie tried to stand. Tried to separate herself from him, but he put out his arm and refused to let her rise.

"I think they are well. I haven't seen them for more than four years."

"Why? You were always so close."

"That changed when I… married. They didn't approve of the man who was my husband."

Livie turned her head. She couldn't let him look at her. Couldn't let him look into her eyes. Theo always understood her better than anyone else.

"Why didn't they approve of him?"

"You've asked enough questions about my personal life."

"I didn't realize asking after your parents was such an intrusion."

"Well, it is! You have no right to ask about things that no longer concern you."

"I see. Then what can I ask you about?"

"Nothing! Absolutely nothing! But, I would like to ask you several questions, Theo. For instance, why did you leave without saying goodbye?"

Theo was silent for several long moments before he spoke. "I didn't have a choice. My father threatened to send me to be trained as a vicar. He threatened to set me up in a parish and force me to live my life behind a pulpit. And he would have done it. I had to escape before morning and there was a ship sailing that night for the war."

"So you left without saying goodbye."

"Yes. I'm not proud of what I did, Livie, but I couldn't have lived the life of a clergyman. You know that."

Livie clutched her hands in her lap. Theo was right. He couldn't have survived the life of a country pastor.

Livie pushed herself to her feet and stepped away from him. "I have work to do. I need to get back to my books. I can't ignore the ledgers."

"Why won't you give me the papers and the jewel, Livie?"

"I told you. I don't have them. How many times do I have to tell you that?"

As many times as you want, Livie. But I won't believe you. You have them. I know you do."

"No, you don't. You don't know anything."

"Do you realize the danger you're in? The French won't give up until they get their items back."

Livie turned her back on him. "Mrs. Barnes should be in the kitchen soon. I need to talk with her. I'm sure she has a list of supplies she needs from town."

Livie took two steps toward the door then stopped. "And you need to help Frank get the wagon ready to go after the items she needs."

Theo rose to his feet. "You're right, Livie. There's much to do."

When she turned to leave, Theo caught her arm. "I'm sorry, Livie. I didn't mean to ask you so many questions. I didn't mean to upset you."

"That was never your intent, but you always managed to do it anyway. I won't let you upset me ever again."

And Livie left him, along with a large part of her heart.

THEO SPENT THE next couple of hours cleaning the stable and caring for the horses. He worked until the muscles across his back and down his arms burned like they were on fire. And he found no relief from the predicament Livie put him in.

Why on earth wouldn't she give him the papers and the jewel? He knew she had them. He knew somehow she'd got her hands on them, yet she wouldn't give them over to him. Why?

He crossed his arms over the railing in one of the stalls and rested his forehead on his forearms. The only reason he could come up with for refusing to give them over to him was because she didn't trust him. And why should she? He'd never given her a reason to trust him. He'd done nothing to earn her trust. If anything, he'd abandoned her and left her to manage on her own after he'd left her.

What reason did she have to trust him after what he'd done?

He let his mind wander in search of answers to the questions he couldn't answer. Suddenly, he heard a muffled sound coming from the rear of the stable. He pushed himself up and reached for the pitchfork he'd propped in the corner and gripped it as he would a weapon.

"Are you going to use that on me?"

"Jack?"

"Yes, it's me."

"Oh, am I glad to see you," Theo whispered huskily.

"Have you found the papers and the jewel?" Jack asked.

Theo breathed a heavy sigh. "Yes, and no."

"What do you mean, yes and no?"

"Yes, I know who has them, but no, I don't know where they're at."

"You care to explain that?" Jack said coming closer.

"I'm sure Livie has them, but she denies she knows anything about them."

"Who is this Livie?"

Theo raked his fingers through his hair, then turned to face Jack. "Livie's a woman I knew before I joined the army. I was going to ask her to marry me, then the war in the Crimea broke out and when my father discovered I wanted to go overseas and fight, he threatened to send me to train for the ministry."

"You!" Jack laughed. "Your father thought you would be a good candidate to occupy a pulpit in a small parish in a country church?"

"Yes. But I knew I would rather die than become a vicar, so I stole aboard the first ship leaving London and joined Her Majesty's army."

"She's not the only woman to bid a soldier farewell as they went to war."

"It wasn't that. I left without telling her I was leaving, or even telling her goodbye."

"That wasn't very noble of you, but you weren't the first man to heed the call of war and you won't be the last."

"Maybe not, but I regret leaving Livie without even a word of farewell."

"And you think this Livie has the papers and the jewels?"

"Yes. But she refuses to tell me where she's hidden them."

"Have you explained how important they are, and how desperate the French are to have them back in their possession?"

"Yes, but rather than tell me where they're hidden, she insists she doesn't have them."

"Has she given you a reason for her refusal to hand them over?"

Theo shook his head.

"Then perhaps I need to speak with her."

Theo glared at Jack with a warning look in his eyes. "You can speak with her, but you will not harm her."

"There's no need to fear, Theo. When have you known me to ever hurt a woman?"

Theo knew abusing women wasn't in Jack's nature, but possession of the jewel and papers was too important to take chances.

"Very well. You may speak to her. But I will be with you

when you do."

"If you insist," Jack said with a smile on his face.

"I do."

"Very well. Ask to meet with her after everyone's retired for the night."

Theo nodded. "What are you going to do now?"

"I'm going to scout the area and see if the French have arrived yet."

"You sound like you expect them any moment."

"Don't you?"

Theo didn't answer Jack, but he knew if the French weren't in the area, they would be soon."

"I'll return when it's dark. Until then, continue as if it is a normal day."

Jack left and Theo did just as Jack ordered him to do. He worked as if it were a normal day and nothing unusual had happened. But if this was normal, he didn't want to experience a day that wasn't normal.

✦

CHAPTER NINE

"**I** THOUGHT I'D find you still up," Theo said from the open doorway. "I'd like to speak with you."

Livie looked up and saw the serious expression on Theo's face and placed her pen beside the ledger she'd been working on. "Very well, Theo. Come in."

Theo entered the room and the first wave of alarm struck her. A second man followed Theo into the room. A man she'd never seen before. A man equally as tall and broad-shouldered as Theo. A man more threatening.

"Livie, this is Major Jack Washburn. Jack, this is Mrs. Olivia Matthews She's in charge of The Angel's Wings Orphanage and Foundling Home."

"Major," Livie greeted.

"Mrs. Matthews," the stranger greeted in return. "Theo tells me it's probable that you have the papers and the jewel our agent took from the French."

Every nerve in Livie's body tightened and her temper soared. "And I told Captain Dunworthy he's incorrect. I don't have them."

The man standing before her had an exceedingly handsome face and his accusations were accompanied by a pleasing voice and friendly smile. But the stern glare in his eyes indicated anything but.

"For argument's sake, let's assume you are lying, and you do have them. But you refuse to hand them over."

"I don't—"

"Please, Mrs. Matthews. Please, humor me and pretend you know the whereabouts of the papers and the jewel. I'm not asking you to hand them over to me, although that is what I'd eventually like you to do, but for now I'm just asking you for information. The first question I'd like answered is, how did you gain possession of the items in question?"

Livie knew she couldn't answer the questioner. She couldn't rise to the bait of his questions. It would be the same as admitting she had the papers and jewel.

Livie looked at the unrelenting expression on the major's face. He wasn't as forgiving as Theo. Although he appeared friendlier on the outside, he would push her much further than Theo had. He would use everything at his disposal to pick away at her until she admitted that she had the papers and the jewel.

If Theo weren't here to stop his friend, she was uncertain of the tactics he would use to force her to reveal the truth. And, she knew once she answered his questions, he'd know she had the papers and the jewel and he'd force her to hand them over. Theo was running out of time and he needed to apply as much pressure as he could. And yet…

Livie remembered the promise she'd made the man who was dying. She had promised she would not give the papers and the jewel to anyone other than Jason. She hadn't promised him that she wouldn't reveal how she got them, only that she wouldn't give them over.

Livie was so tired of lying to Theo. It had gone on long enough. It was time to tell someone what she knew.

"Please, sit down," she said, indicating the two chairs that sat before her desk.

Theo and the other man sat.

"I was on my way to my cottage one evening and I stumbled upon an injured man. He'd been shot. He was dying."

"Did he tell you his name?"

Livie shook her head. "He was too injured."

"What happened?"

"He… He gave me the papers and the jewel and told me to hide them. He made me promise that I wouldn't give the papers or the jewel to anyone except a man called Jason."

"Jason?" Theo and Jack said in unison. "Are you sure he said Jason?"

"That's what he said."

"Do you know anyone named Jason, Jack?"

"No. I don't know anyone by that name in the agency."

"What do you suppose he meant?" Theo asked his friend.

"I don't know. What else did he say, Mrs. Matthews?"

"Nothing else. He just repeated what I told you. Except, he told me there was a traitor in your agency and I couldn't trust anyone else. He made me promise I wouldn't give the papers or the jewel to anyone except Jason."

Theo rose to his feet and walked away from her, then poured a glass of wine then handed it to her. "Drink this. You need it."

Livie took a sip of the wine then set her glass on the desk. Theo knelt before her and leveled her with the harshest look imaginable. He reached for her hands in her lap and squeezed her fingers.

"You can't keep the papers and the jewel, Livie," he said. "The French won't let you. They'll come for them and force you to hand them over."

Livie shook her head. "They don't know I have them."

"You don't know that. You can't be sure."

Livie pulled her hands out of Theo's grasp. "I can't hand them over to you, Theo. I promised a dying man that I wouldn't."

"You won't be safe until you give them to us, Livie. The French want the papers and jewel too desperately. They won't stop until they have them."

Thankfully Major Washburn stopped Theo's interrogation. "That's enough, Theo. Mrs. Matthews has told us what she knows. We're done now."

Theo breathed a heavy sigh of frustration and walked away from her.

"I can't, Theo. Don't you understand? I promised a dying man that I wouldn't give anyone but a man called Jason what he'd given me."

"Which means you don't trust me," Theo said with an angry look.

"It's not about trust," Livie whispered as she reached for her glass of wine and held it in her hands. "It's about keeping my word."

Theo walked to the window and stared out into the blackness. "Go to bed, Livie. It's late. You don't need to stay up any longer."

"What about you, Theo?"

"I'm not tired."

"What about you, Major Washburn?"

"I'll be along later. I just want to tour the grounds first."

"Are you expecting trouble?"

"No," Theo said turning from the window. "But it doesn't hurt to make sure everything is calm out there."

"Good night, then," Livie said. "Show Major Washburn a room when you're ready to retire," she said and left the room. She was terribly tired, but she wasn't sure she could sleep. She hadn't slept well since Theo had shown up all those weeks ago. As always, he was still the cause of her sleepless nights.

❯❯❯❮❮❮

A WEEK HAD gone by since Jack had arrived. "What are you showing me?" Jack asked as Theo led him through a copse of trees and across a shallow stream.

Theo stopped, then climbed a small rise. When he reached the top, he stopped and pointed to the north. "Do you see it?"

Jack looked in the direction that Theo pointed. "Bloody hell. How long have they been there?"

"I noticed them two days ago." Theo sat in the tall grass and kept his gaze focused on the small campfires that dotted the horizon. "I estimate that there are twenty to thirty of them."

"Do you think they're after the papers and the jewel?" Jack said, watching the French soldiers set up camp near the opposite side of the stream.

"I don't know what else they could be after. I think they followed Wallace here, then lost his trail."

"It won't be long now before they make their move." Jack pulled his binoculars from a bag hanging over his saddle and focused on the enemy soldiers.

"What do you see?" Theo asked.

"It's still early and only a few of them are moving. In an hour or two the whole camp will be awake. Then they'll make their first move."

"Livie won't be safe once they realize she has what they are after," Theo said, then pushed himself to his feet and headed back to where they'd left the horses.

"What are you going to do?" Jack asked.

Theo raked his fingers through his hair. "I'm not sure what I can do," he said when they reached their horses. "Livie's so damn stubborn she'll never give the papers and jewel up until the man called Jason comes."

"What if there isn't anyone called Jason?"

"There is. We just have to hope he shows up before the French come after what she's hiding."

THE DAYS WEREN'T nearly as chilly as they'd been earlier. Livie was finally able to escape her office and the endless work on the ledgers to take a walk in the sunshine. Today was a perfect day for her to get out and walk across the meadow. It was also one of the few days she'd been able to escape Theo's watchful eye. He and Jack guarded her every movement as if they hoped she would lead them to the papers and the jewel.

Even though Theo warned her to stay inside the orphanage and not venture anywhere outside or alone, she knew they were only being overprotective.

Livie wasn't afraid anything would happen. She only wished the man named Jason would arrive so she could fulfill the promise she'd made to the man who'd died in her arms. She'd kept the papers and the jewel hidden for almost two months now and was losing all hope that anyone would come to rescue them.

She walked across the meadow, then neared the stream. It had been so long since she'd been here. She forgot how relaxing this place was. She forgot how much she enjoyed the peaceful atmosphere. Livie leaned back against a large shade tree and closed her eyes. She needed to think. She needed to remember how much she loved Theo, and how much she enjoyed being with him.

She closed her eyes and tilted her head back. She was nearly asleep when the loud snapping of a tree limb startled her awake.

Livie opened her eyes and turned her head as two French officers pulled her to her feet and clasped her arms in an iron grip.

She tried to scream, but the soldiers wrapped a cloth around her mouth making it impossible for her to utter a sound. Four more French soldiers surrounded her and the group of soldiers dragged her through the trees.

Livie struggled to get away, but her efforts to escape were met with two hard slaps across her face. She wasn't sure where they were taking her but the harder she fought, the more violent her captors became. Finally, they reached the French army camp and the French soldiers shoved her inside a tent. Before she regained her balance, the soldiers slammed her against the center pole and tied her hands above her head.

She turned her head when there was a rustling near the opening of the tent and a highly decorated officer stepped before her.

She tried to move but it was impossible.

"Struggling will do you no good," the officer said and he removed the cloth around her mouth. "We do not intend for you to escape."

"What do you want?" Livie said trying to sound as innocent as possible.

"You know what we want. We want the papers the Englishman stole from us and a very valuable jewel."

"I don't know what you're talking about," Livie answered but before she could finish her sentence, the officer's fist swung out and clipped her on the jaw.

"Don't play games with me, madam. You know exactly what I'm talking about."

"But I don't. I have no idea what you're talking about."

Before Livie was barely finished with her sentence, the officer reached out and hit her again.

"Where are they?" he demanded again.

"I can't give you what you want. I don't have any papers or a jewel."

The officer's fist swung out again.

Livie's face throbbed and her eyes blurred. Her right eye was beginning to swell and she couldn't see out of it clearly.

The officer gripped her chin between his thumb and forefinger and squeezed tight.

Livie tried not to react, but she couldn't stop a whimper of pain from escaping.

"The pain is only going to get worse, madam. I want those papers and that jewel. I refuse to give up until you tell me where they are at."

"I don't know. I don't know what you're talking about."

The French officer's fist made contact with her jaw once more, then he turned to one of his officers and ordered him to turn her around so her back was to him. Before she had time to prepare herself for what was going to happen, the French officer ripped her gown down her back and took a step away from her.

His hand reached for the whip hanging from his belt and he brought the whip down with a snap.

Livie's back arched and she let out a muffled cry. The burning pain was greater than any pain she'd ever felt before. She didn't know how she would endure what was to come. She didn't know if she was brave enough.

Before she was prepared, the officer's arm pulled back and the whip tore another stripe in her skin.

"Where are they, madam? Where are the papers and the jewel?"

"I don't know," Livie said, even though she knew her answer would cause her more pain.

If the man who gave her the papers and the jewel was willing to die to protect them, she would have to do the same.

Livie closed her eyes and let Theo's face appear before her. She loved him. He was the only man she would ever love. The only man who would ever possess her heart.

"Where are they?" the French commander bellowed.

"I don't know."

"You are going to tell me, or you will die with their hiding place on your lips."

"I don't know," she said as forcefully as she could manage.

The whip came down again and again, and she concentrated on Theo's face, his voice, his touch. Darkness consumed her as she remembered Theo's kiss. His body enveloping hers as they made love.

CHAPTER TEN

"M ARIE?"

"Yes, Captain Dunworthy."

"Have you seen Mrs. Matthews lately?"

"No, Captain. Not since earlier this afternoon."

Theo walked to the foyer and opened the front door. It was unlike Livie to leave the children in the middle of the afternoon. Unlike her to be gone so long, and according to everyone he'd talked to, no one had seen her since before lunch.

He increased his speed as he left the orphanage and headed for the stable. Jack should have been back by now. He'd left earlier to spy on the French army. He and Jack took turns watching the movement of the French troops. The fact that they hadn't left meant something. It meant that they didn't have the papers or the jewel and couldn't leave until they did. Theo knew they were running out of time and getting more desperate to get their hands on the papers and jewel.

"Jack," Theo called out.

"I'm here, Theo. I was just coming to get you."

"What have you found?"

"Something is going on. The French have been put on alert."

"What do you think that means?"

"I'm not sure. I think we need to check it out."

"You didn't happen to see Livie on your way back, did you?"

"No. Isn't she here?"

"No one's seen her all afternoon."

A wave of terror consumed him. Even though he told her to stay inside and not venture away from the orphanage, he knew her well enough to know she hadn't taken his warnings seriously. She honestly thought that no one knew she might have the papers and the jewel. She was confident that she was safe.

But she wasn't.

Theo's heart beat faster and louder. It pounded in his throat and in his chest. He was so scared, he thought he might be ill.

"Come on, Jack. We need to check the French camp."

"You think they might have her?" Jack asked as he saddled his horse.

"We need to make sure they don't."

Theo and Jack rode in the direction of the French army camp and stopped in the copse of trees where he and Jack couldn't be seen. They crouched behind a bush and Theo took out his binoculars.

"Do you see the far tent on the right?" Theo asked.

"Yes. Something is happening there. There's a great deal of activity going on around it."

"Cover me," Theo said. "I'm going to go around the back and see what has drawn everyone's attention."

"I'll be right behind you," Jack whispered.

Theo made his way to the tent where something was going on, then stopped to make sure he hadn't been spotted. When he was sure no one had seen him, he crawled toward the back of the tent and lifted the canvas so he could get a look inside. His heart skipped a beat and a rock dropped to the pit of his stomach when he saw inside.

Livie's arms were stretched above her head and she was tied to a pole in the center of the tent. The back of her gown had been ripped from her neck to her waist and blood streamed down her back.

She'd been whipped. From her limp body and the way her

head hung to her chest, Theo wasn't sure she was even alive. Fingers of dread wrapped around his heart and squeezed until he couldn't breathe. His legs threatened to give out beneath him.

He wanted to rush into the tent and free her, but Jack's fingers clasped on his shoulder to keep him in place.

"Keep your head, Theo. There are two guards watching her. We have to get rid of them first."

Theo knew Jack was correct. He knew rushing in would only get him killed.

"You take the one on the right," Theo whispered, "and I'll take the one on the left."

Jack nodded and they cut the canvas and rushed into the tent. Theo hit the soldier on the left and he crumpled to the ground and Jack did the same to the soldier on the right. They cut the ropes that held Livie's hands and Theo caught her limp body when she crumpled to the ground.

"I have you now, Livie. I have you, sweetheart."

He picked her up and Livie moaned in pain. He cradled her in his arms and whispered in her ear. "You're alright, Livie. I have you. I'll take care of you."

Theo followed Jack out of the tent the way they'd entered. Livie came to when she was jostled.

"I didn't tell them anything... Theo. I didn't tell them... where the papers and the... jewel were... at."

"I know, Livie. I know you didn't."

"I didn't tell them," she mumbled in a weak voice.

Theo brushed the hair from Livie's face and kissed her forehead. "Stay with me, Livie."

"I can't."

"Yes, you can. You're one of the strongest women I know."

They made their way as quickly as they could to where their horses were tied.

"If something happens to me—"

"Nothing is going to happen to you. You'll be much better when we get you back to the orphanage."

Jack helped Theo mount with Livie in his arms.

"Promise you'll… take care of him. Please… Don't let him… grow up… alone."

"Who, Livie?"

"Jamie. Jamie. Don't let him… grow up… alone."

"I'll take care of him, Livie. You don't have to worry about him."

When they were settled atop the horse, they made their way back. When they reached the orphanage, Theo carried Livie up the stairs and to her room. She moaned with every step he took but he couldn't stop or slow down.

"Bring me some water and clean cloths," he yelled and several of the staff ran to follow his orders. "Watch for any movement by the French, Jack."

"I will. You take care of her," Jack said, checking the view from the two windows in the room.

Theo placed Livie on the bed and pulled her gown away so he could clean her wounds.

"Bloody hell," he hissed when he saw what they'd done to her.

"Theo," Livie whispered in a ragged voice. "The papers are… safe. I didn't tell them… anything."

"Don't talk, sweetheart. Save your strength."

"I'm sorry. I should have… given them to… you."

Theo ran cool water over her back and dabbed at the pools of blood that were running from each open cut.

"I'm sorry," he said when he placed the rag in his hands on one of the deeper cuts and Livie moaned out loud.

"I'm… all right, Theo. I can hardly feel anything."

"Good, Livie. I'm glad," Theo answered, but he knew she was lying. He'd been flogged more than once and knew the pain he'd endured was horrific. It was a pain that didn't lessen but continued to burn like fire.

"Here," he said holding a glass of brandy to her lips. "Take a swallow of this." He'd added a bit of laudanum to the brandy.

Hopefully, it would help ease the pain.

Livie took a swallow of the pain reliever and slowly relaxed. Her breathing slowed and became more shallow. Instead of making him feel more at ease, her shallow breathing caused a nagging concern to grow inside his chest.

"Livie," he said, clasping his hands on her shoulders.

She didn't answer him. Her body was limp when he tried to move her. She'd stopped breathing.

"Livie! Livie! Come back to me! You cannot leave me. I won't let you!"

Theo lifted her and held her against him. She wasn't breathing. She'd gone deathly still.

Theo opened her mouth and clasped his mouth over hers and started breathing for her. He placed his hand beneath her breasts and pressed down with each breath he took, like he'd seen one of the doctors do when a soldier had stopped breathing.

Again and again he breathed for her, willing her to come back to him. "Breathe, Livie! Breathe, damn it!

He took a breath for her again and again, until he realized she was breathing on her own.

"She's back, Theo," Jack said from behind him. "She's breathing."

Theo wiped the tears that were running down his cheeks and cradled Livie in his arms. He'd nearly lost her and he wasn't sure what he'd do if he did. He wasn't sure he could survive without her. He needed her too badly. Now that he'd found her again, he wasn't sure he could live if she wasn't in his world.

Theo lowered her onto the bed and straightened the covers over her. He kept her back exposed and applied some of the salve Mrs. Barnes had sent up. When he had her settled, he sat in the chair next to the bed.

"She's back," Jack repeated. "That was close." He sat in the chair next to Theo.

"Is there any sign of the French?"

"No, but a currier just brought a message from Commander

Waterford. He should be here in less than an hour."

"Good. We'll need his help if the French come for the papers and the jewel."

Theo rinsed a cloth in the fresh water Marie just brought into the room and wiped Livie's back. When he dried her skin, he applied more of the salve Mrs. Barnes had sent up for her wounds.

"Why don't you go below and wait for Waterford. Bring him up when he arrives. I'd come down but I'm not going to leave her," Theo said, still applying the salve.

"Right."

Theo nodded and watched Jack leave the room.

"I need you to stay with me, Livie," Theo said, holding her hand. "I can't lose you. You're too important to me."

Theo wasn't sure when it had happened. He'd always loved her. At least a part of him had cared for Livie unlike he'd ever cared for any woman before, but almost losing her caused him to realize how all-consuming that love was. Almost losing her showed him how empty his life would be without her.

"I can't lose you, Livie. You're the reason I live. The only reason."

Livie didn't answer, but lay on the bed with her eyes closed and her breathing shallow. She was far from out of danger. The French had beat her within an inch of her life. Theo would make them pay if it was the last thing he did.

THEO SAT AT Livie's bedside and when she was restless, he whispered comforting words to her and told her over and over that he loved her and refused to allow her to leave him.

She went in and out of consciousness, but even when she was awake, her thoughts seemed to be confused. Several times she asked for the man called Jason. She was adamant in her demand that he come to see her.

Then, she cried out for someone called Jamie. Theo thought perhaps Jamie might be one of the children at the orphanage, but how could that be? Why had she chosen that particular child to be so concerned over?

"Theo," she called out.

"Yes, sweetheart. What is it?"

"Promise me that you'll take care of him. Please."

"Who are you talking about, Livie?"

"Jamie. Promise me… you'll take… care… of him. Please."

"Of course I will, sweetheart. I'll take care of him. Is Jamie here? Is he one of the children?"

"Oh, Theo," she whimpered. "Promise you won't let anything happen to him."

"I promise, Livie. But you don't need to worry. You'll be here to take care of him."

Livie's head thrashed from side to side.

"Yes, you will!" Theo said in a firm voice. "Don't you dare leave me. Do you hear me?"

"Jamie," she mumbled. "Jamie."

Theo rose to his feet and went to the door. "Marie," he called out and Marie rushed into the room. "Livie's calling out for someone called Jamie. Do you know who she wants to see?"

"Yes, Captain."

"Get him. Bring him here."

"Yes, Captain," she answered and rushed to the children's rooms.

"He's coming, Livie. Jamie's coming. Marie's getting him."

"Jamie," she mumbled as tears ran from her eyes to the pillow beneath her.

Theo placed cool cloths on her back then more salve. He stopped when the door opened and Marie entered with a little boy about four years old. His gaze focused on Theo, then shifted to where Livie lay on the bed. When he saw her, he raced to her side and reached for her.

"Mama! Oh, Mama!"

CHAPTER ELEVEN

"MAMA!" JAMIE CRIED out again.

Theo caught him before he touched Livie and picked him up and sat him on his lap.

"Jamie?" Theo asked in disbelief.

"That's my mama," he cried as tears filled his eyes and ran down his cheeks. "What's wrong with her?"

"Your mama's had an accident. Why don't you kneel down beside the bed so your mama can see you?"

The boy slid from Theo's lap and knelt beside the bed. He reached for Livie's hand and held it. "Mama, wake up. Please, Mama. Wake up."

"Jamie?" Livie asked with a smile on her face.

"Yes, Mama."

"Don't cry, Jamie. Everything is all right."

"Who hurt you?"

"No one, Jamie. I had… an accident."

"Will you be all right?"

"Yes, sweetheart. I'll be… fine."

"I brought Ralph with me," he said. "Would you like him to sleep with you? He'll make you feel better."

"I'd like that," Livie answered and Jamie placed his stuffed bear next to her.

"Thank you, sweetheart. I feel better… already."

"I knew you would. Ralph always makes me feel better when I'm afraid."

"You be a good boy until I'm better and mind Marie and Theo."

"I will, Mama," he said, then stopped and reached for her hand. "Mama? Mama?"

"She's sleeping, Jamie. You have to let her rest."

"What happened to her?" Livie's son asked as he stared at Theo. Big tears spilled from his eyes and ran down his cheeks.

Theo stared at the boy in front of him and a large boulder pressed against his heart.

Theo felt as if he was looking in a mirror and seeing a younger version of himself. The boy's hair was the same dark brown as his own, his eyes were the same shade of midnight blue. He even had the cleft in his chin that was a trait of the males in his family.

"Your mama said your name was Jamie. Is that right?"

"Yes. It's really James Theodore, but mama calls me Jamie."

Theo's eyes closed tight as if he were trying to take this in and couldn't quite. "How old are you, Jamie?"

"Four. But I'll be five in the summertime."

"Where's your father?"

"I don't have one. He died before I was born. Mama said she'd tell me about him when I got older."

Theo sank back in his chair and stared at the boy beside Livie's bed. Jamie was his son. Now that he knew it, the resemblance was remarkable.

"Have you been here a long time?" Theo asked.

"Uh-huh. Mama said I was born here."

Another stabbing pain hit him in the gut. Theo turned his gaze to where Livie lay on the bed. What had he done to her? What had she endured because he'd abandoned her?

"Can we wake Mama up? I want to talk to her."

"No, Jamie. We need to let your mama sleep. She's very tired." Theo reached for his son's hand and held it. "I think you should leave now so your mama can get some rest. You can come again later."

"Is she going to be alright?" his son asked.

"Yes, your mama is going to be fine. I promise." Theo touched his son's soft cheek and brushed the wetness that was still there. "I'll find Marie and she can take you back to your room."

Theo stood on legs that threatened to give out beneath him and opened the door to the hall. Marie was waiting for him and she took Jamie's hand.

"When can I visit my mama again?" he asked turning around to stare at Theo.

"Soon, Jamie. Soon. Marie can bring you back before dinner."

Theo watched his son walk down the hall and he couldn't put a name to the feelings that assaulted him. He had a son, a son he never knew existed.

"Who was that?" Jack asked when he reached Theo.

"That's my son," Theo answered.

"What?"

"That's my son. A son I didn't know I had."

Theo looked at the shock and disbelief on Jack's face, then raked his fingers through his hair and returned to Livie's bedside. Jack followed him inside.

"How is she?" he asked when they were in the room.

"Alive. I need to give her some more laudanum. She's in a great deal of pain."

Theo poured some wine into a glass, then added a little laudanum. When he finished, he lifted the glass to her lips and forced her to drink.

"A courier just arrived. Commander Waterford is almost here. He'll demand the papers and the jewel."

"Well, he won't get them. Livie's in no condition to talk to him."

"Waterford won't care what condition she's in," Jack said, looking out the window. "He's desperate to get his hands on whatever Wallace gave her."

"If only Livie would have trusted me," Theo said. He sat on the edge of the bed and brushed Livie's hair from her face, then placed a cool cloth on her neck. She stirred when he touched her.

"Livie, stay still. Don't move."

Theo placed his hands on her arms to hold her down.

"Theo," she cried out.

"Yes, Livie. Just lay still."

"I didn't… give them the… papers or the… jewel."

"I know, sweetheart."

"I… promised… I wouldn't."

"I know, Livie. I know."

"Where are they now, Mrs. Matthews?" Jack asked. "Where are they?"

"I… hid them."

"I need them, Livie," Theo said.

"No. I can't."

"Who did you promise you would give them to?"

"Jason," she whispered. "I can only give them… to Jason."

"I don't know a Jason. I don't think there is anyone by that name."

"Only… Jason," she slurred. "Only… Jason."

Livie closed her eyes and fell asleep.

Theo turned to Jack. "Do you know anyone called Jason?"

Jack shook his head. "No. We don't have anyone in the agency called Jason."

Just then there was a knock on the door and Marie entered. "Captain. Some men have arrived. They want to speak to you. I showed them to Mrs. Matthews' study."

"Thank you, Marie. Would you stay with Livie until I return?"

"Of course."

Theo and Jack went down to meet with Commander Waterford. When they entered the room there was another officer in the room with him.

"Captain Dunworthy. Major Washburn. Allow me to present

Commander McBride. He has come to take over my command."

"You are stepping down?" Jack asked.

"As soon as the papers and the jewel are in our possession, I am being transferred. From now on you will receive your orders from Commander McBride."

"It's a pleasure to meet you, Commander," Theo said and Jack seconded his greeting.

"Now, Captain," Commander Waterford said. "Fill us in on the details. Do you have the papers and the jewel in your possession?"

"No, Commander. We don't."

"Who does?" Commander McBride asked.

"Mrs. Matthews does."

"Where is she? We'll need to talk to her right away."

"I'm afraid that's impossible, sir. She was captured by the French and tortured in an attempt to get the items you want."

"Did she reveal where they were?"

"No, sir. She did not. Even though she was tortured in their effort to get her to reveal where they were."

"Where is she now?" Commander McBride asked.

"Upstairs, Sir. We are caring for her."

"Are her wounds serious?" McBride asked.

"Yes, Sir. Very. We are trying to keep her alive. It's not certain she will survive."

This was the first time Theo had said out loud how serious Livie's wounds were. The first time he'd admitted how close to dying she was.

"Perhaps we could go up and talk to her," Commander McBride said. "I promise we will not tire her any more than necessary."

"Is that wise?" Waterford said. "If she's injured as badly as Captain Dunworthy says—"

"I promise we won't tax her overly much," Commander McBride interrupted.

"Perhaps for a moment, then," Waterford said in a terse

voice. It was obvious he wasn't pleased with McBride's insistence that he talk to Mrs. Matthews.

"We'll only need a moment," McBride insisted.

"Follow me," Theo said, and led Waterford and McBride up the stairs.

Something was wrong. Theo sensed a friction between Waterford and McBride. Waterford's removal from this case was too abrupt. McBride's orders too curt. It was as if the two were battling for control of the leadership position. As if Waterford didn't want McBride to gain possession of the papers or the jewel.

Almost as if Waterford didn't trust the new commander. Or if McBride didn't trust Waterford.

When they reached Livie's room the two commanders entered, but they didn't attempt to talk to Livie. She was still unconscious.

"Have you searched her room, Captain?" Commander Waterford asked.

"Yes, but I didn't find anything."

McBride took a last look at Livie. "We won't be able to talk to her until she's gained consciousness," he said, then walked to the door. He left the room and returned to Livie's study. Waterford followed along with Theo and Jack.

"Would you care for a brandy?" Theo asked.

"Yes," McBride said, sitting in one of the chairs before the fire.

"Nothing for me," Waterford said. "I need to get back to my men. I'll send a few men to keep watch. I don't trust the French."

"I think I'll stay here, if you don't mind," McBride answered. "I'd like to ask you a few questions, and I want to be on hand when Mrs. Matthews wakes."

"Of course," Theo answered. "There's a spare room above stairs where you can sleep."

Theo walked Waterford through the foyer. The commander stopped when he reached the door.

"Keep an eye on Mrs. Matthews, Captain. She's in danger as

long as she has the papers and the jewel."

"I will, Sir."

"Let me know if you need any assistance."

"I will, Sir. Thank you." Theo turned to Waterford. "Is every-thing all right, Commander?"

"I'm not sure," Waterford answered then he left.

Theo stood for a moment trying unsuccessfully to digest what Waterford meant with his words, then he returned to Livie's study.

"What did Mrs. Matthews tell you about the papers and the jewel?" McBride asked when they were alone in the study.

"She said she found our agent. He'd been severely wounded and was dying. He gave her the items before he died and made her promise that she wouldn't hand the items over to anyone except a man called Jason."

"You're sure she said Jason."

"Yes. She said he expressly told her not to give the jewel and papers to anyone except Jason. He also told her that we have a traitor in our agency."

McBride paused long enough to take a swallow of his liquor. "Did she say who Frank thought this traitor was?"

"No."

McBride rose from his chair and paced the room. Theo looked at Jack and saw the confused expression on his face. Theo felt the same.

McBride stopped pacing and turned to face them. "The man's name was Frank Wallace. He was my partner. I am the man he was talking about. My name is Commander Jason McBride. I'm an agent in Her Majesty's service."

"Do you know who this traitor is?" Theo asked.

"I have an idea. But nothing I can prove."

Jack finished the liquor in his glass and sat forward. "Who do you think it is?"

"I'm pretty sure it's Commander Waterford."

"Commander Waterford!" Jack and Theo said in disbelief.

"Yes. All signs point to him."

"I can't believe Waterford would betray England."

"It's amazing what people will do for money. And that jewel alone is worth a king's ransom."

"But Waterford has always been a loyal citizen."

"Like I said," Commander McBride said, taking a sip of his brandy. "All facts point to him, but so far I can't prove them. Just keep your eye on him. We don't want him to get to Mrs. Matthews. If she's the only one who knows the whereabouts of the papers and the jewel, our traitor is going to have to try to get her to reveal where she has them hidden."

Theo shook his head. "That won't happen. The French nearly beat her to death and she wouldn't tell them."

"But they didn't have the leverage that's here," Jack said.

Theo and McBride turned to Jack. "What leverage?"

"The children, Theo. One in particular."

Theo raked his fingers through his hair. "Bloody Hell."

"Explain yourself, Washburn."

"Livie and I share a past, Commander," Theo said, needing to explain the situation himself. "We had a son together. He's here."

"I see," the commander said then rose to his feet. "That presents a problem, then."

"Yes, especially if our traitor discovers your secret," Jack said, looking at Theo.

"Yes," Theo answered, clenching the arms of his chair until his fingers ached. "Threatening our son is the only thing that will cause Livie to break her promise."

McBride turned to face Theo. "Then we need to make sure that never happens. We need to make sure our traitor never gets his hands on your son.

CHAPTER TWELVE

THEO SAT AT Livie's bedside and watched Livie's back rise and fall with her breathing. She'd nearly died protecting the papers' and jewel's hiding place. He couldn't explain the emotions that raged through him. He loved her more than he thought possible. He'd fallen in love with her when he'd first met her nearly five years ago. And he loved her just as much today. Even more.

He rinsed a cloth in clean, cool water and placed it on Livie's back. She shifted beneath him and moaned.

"Don't move," he whispered. "You'll tear open your wounds and start bleeding again."

"Theo?"

"Yes, Livie. I'm here. I'll always be here. I'll never leave you again."

"Are you all right?"

"Am *I* all right? Theo asked.

He smiled. He wanted to laugh. She was laying on the bed with bleeding welts covering her back and she wanted to know if he was all right. "Yes, sweetheart. I'm fine."

"The children?"

"Yes. They're fine, too." Theo leaned closer to whisper in her ear. "Jason is here."

"Jason?"

"Yes, Jason. His name is Jason McBride. He's a commander in Her Majesty's service."

"Oh," she sighed.

"He'd like to talk to you. Are you up to talking to him for a while?"

"Yes."

Livie's voice was weak, but she seemed a little stronger than she'd been yesterday.

"Livie, I want you to do something for me." Theo sat beside her on the bed. "Don't ask me why, just do it, all right?"

"Yes. What's wrong?"

"Nothing. I'm just being extra careful."

"All right," she sighed.

"Commander McBride is going to want the papers and the jewel. You can tell him that you know where they are, but don't give them to him yet. Tell him you're the only one who can get them and you're not well enough. Just tell him when you're better you'll give them to him."

"Why, Theo?"

"That's not important. Just do it. Do you understand?"

"Yes."

"Good. Now, I'll go down and bring him up."

Theo left the room and returned with McBride and Jack.

"Livie, this is Commander Jason McBride."

Livie tried to open her eyes, but Theo could see how difficult it was for her to stay awake.

"Mrs. Matthews," the commander said. "It's a pleasure to meet you. Thank you for taking care of my friend, Frank Wallace, and for protecting the papers and jewel he gave you."

"I wish there had been… something I could have… done for… him, but… he'd been injured… too badly."

"I know you did everything you could," McBride said. "Captain Dunworthy tells me he gave you something to give to me."

"Yes, I hid it."

"Would you give it to me now?"

"It's safe. I put it where it's… safe."

"But I'd like to have it, now, Mrs. Matthews. My friend took it so our government could have it."

Livie's eyes opened and she looked at Commander McBride. Theo didn't know what she saw but a frown deepened across her brow and she became agitated."

"The jewel, Mrs. Matthews. Where is it?"

"It's safe, Commander."

"I want it, Mrs. Matthews. It's important that you give it to me. Now."

"It's safe," Livie repeated, then closed her eyes.

"I know it's safe. I just want it. Tell me where it is."

"Theo," she said. There was a desperate tone to her voice.

"Yes, sweetheart. I'm here."

"I don't feel well. I hurt."

"I know you do. Just close your eyes and go to sleep."

"Captain," Commander McBride said in a demanding voice. "I need that jewel. Give me the jewel."

"It's safe, Commander. It's safe," she repeated, then was gone to them.

"I'm afraid she's unconscious, sir," Theo said. He took Livie's hand in his and held it.

"Jack, why don't you take Commander McBride downstairs and get him something to eat. I'll be down in a little while."

"If you'll follow me, Commander," Jack said and led the way down the stairs.

"Livie," Theo said when they were gone. "What is it? What did you see?"

"Something's wrong," Livie whispered softly.

"What is it?" he asked and reached for her hand and held it.

"I don't know. I can't remember," she whispered again, then was asleep.

THEO STAYED WITH Livie for several hours after McBride left her room. Theo knew he wanted the papers and the jewel and was disappointed that Livie hadn't told him where they were, but he'd have to wait until she was stronger. He'd have to wait until Theo was convinced McBride was the man who deserved them. Until then, the location of the papers and the jewel would have to remain a mystery.

Theo held Livie's hand and rubbed her flesh. She'd endured so much even though it wasn't her responsibility to endure any of what she'd gone through. She didn't work for the crown. She shouldn't have had to protect the papers or the jewel. If anyone should have had to, it should have been him. The beating she took should have fallen on him.

Suddenly, she moved as if she'd been grabbed.

"Lay still, Livie. You're all right. You're safe now."

Her eyes opened and she stared at him. "Oh," she moaned.

"What's wrong, sweetheart?" Theo lifted her hand and held it in his, then brushed her hair from her face. "Do you need something for the pain?"

"No. I don't... like the way it makes me feel."

"I know, Livie. But you need to take it. Just until the pain lessons."

She thrashed her head from side to side. Livie's eyes opened and there was a look of terror in her eyes. "Something's wrong, Theo."

"What's wrong, Livie?"

"I can't remember. It's McBride Don't give him the jewel."

"I won't. I won't give him the jewel."

"No, Theo. Don't give him the jewel."

"I won't," Theo whispered in her ear. "Now, go to sleep, Livie."

"Oh, Theo. I know you're angry that I didn't give you the papers and the jewel."

"I wish you had, Livie. It would have saved you from enduring what you went through."

"But they would have tortured you."

"I would have gladly traded places with you."

"It's over now, Theo. Too late for regrets."

Theo rinsed a cloth in the water beside the bed and placed it on Livie's back. She arched the second the water touched her. When he finished, he applied the salve Mrs. Barnes had given them for her welts, then put a few drops of laudanum into her wine and made her drink.

"I need to go below and talk to Jack and the commander. Marie will stay with you."

"I'm fine. Just tired."

"I know, sweetheart. Rest until I return"

"Do you know who the traitor is?"

"No. But we'll find him, Livie. Now, go to sleep."

Theo leaned down and kissed her cheek. She was a strong female. He prayed she would survive this. He didn't know what he'd do if she didn't.

He left Livie's bedroom when Marie came to watch over her, and Theo joined Jack and the commander downstairs. They were deep in conversation when he entered the room.

"Do you have any idea who the traitor might be?" Jack was asking the commander.

"I have my suspicions, but nothing I can prove."

Theo poured himself a glass of brandy, then sat down between the two agents. "Do you have a plan to force the traitor into the open, Commander?"

"Yes, but there's a certain amount of risk involved."

"Risk to whom?" Theo asked.

"Mrs. Matthews."

"No," Theo answered. "She's gone through enough. I won't have her put in any more danger."

"There's not another way, Captain. And we'll be there to protect her."

"You can't guarantee that nothing will happen to her and I won't take the chance that something will."

"What is your plan, Commander?" Jack asked.

"No, Jack!"

"Let's hear him out, Theo. Maybe we can change the commander's plan enough so no one will be in danger."

Theo considered Jack's suggestion. This isn't what he wanted, but maybe they could work with it. "What are you suggesting, Commander?"

"I think we should let it be known that Mrs. Matthews has the items the French want. That she told us that she's hidden them in her room but we haven't been able to find them."

"Why can't we say they are hidden here in her study?" Theo asked.

"Because there are too many entrances to this room. It has two windows, a door leading from the outside, and a door leading from the room next to this one. Her bedroom only has one door and the only way to get to the room is by climbing the stairs. We can watch every move the traitor makes to get to Mrs. Matthews' bedroom and catch him in the act."

Theo considered McBride's plan. It was solid, and he would make sure Livie was safe. They had to catch the thief in the act, or they wouldn't be able to prove who the traitor was.

⇥⇥⇥⇤⇤⇤

SEVERAL DAYS PASSED and McBride let it be known that Livie had the papers and the jewel. Theo and Jack and two other soldiers with McBride kept watch, staying in her room twenty-four hours a day.

Theo was sure that the thief would make his attempt during the night, so he stayed with Livie each night.

The first three nights produced nothing. No one tried to enter the room, nor did anyone enter the orphanage. Theo was sure whoever intended to steal the papers and the jewel didn't want it bad enough to risk getting caught.

"Is that you, Theo?" Livie asked during the fourth night shortly before dawn.

"What are you doing awake, sweetheart?"

"I'm watching to see what you are doing."

"And I'm watching to see what you are doing," Theo answered in return. He saw a smile light her face, thanks to the moonlight.

"Are you waiting for someone to come to try to steal the papers and the jewel?"

"Yes," he answered, looking out the window again.

"When they come," she answered, "they won't find anything. They're not hidden in here."

"They're not?"

"Heavens no. That would be ridiculous. Why would I hide them in the first place anyone would look for them?"

Theo laughed. "Of course not. You'd never make it that easy for a thief."

"Thank you," she answered on a sigh. "But I'm still not going to tell you where they're hidden."

"But what if something were to happen to you?"

"Then I guess no one would ever find them."

"And that wouldn't bother you?"

"No, Theo. Not at all. The papers and that jewel have already taken enough lives. I personally don't care if they're ever found."

The next day, Theo told McBride that the papers and the jewel weren't hidden in Livie's room and he called off watching her room.

The fact that he called off watching Livie's room only reinforced Theo's assumption that McBride wasn't who he claimed to be. He'd also had plenty of opportunity to search Livie's room and hadn't found anything, so he knew the papers and jewel weren't hidden there. It also proved that McBride was still a suspect as the traitor.

And as long as he thought McBride couldn't be trusted, he knew Livie wasn't safe. She needed to be constantly watched for her own protection.

⟫⟫⟫✦⟪⟪⟪

LIVIE HEALED MORE each day. She was finally healed enough to leave her room and look in on the children, or go to her study and work on the ledgers, at least for an hour. Theo stayed close by her all the time, both to protect her and to be near her. He needed to make sure she didn't overdo it.

"Don't you think you've been up long enough, Livie?" he asked her the third day she was up. "You look tired."

"I'm fine, Theo. I need to stay up longer to build up my strength. I've been in bed long enough. And I want to stop in to see Jamie and Lady Dianna's baby girl before I go to my room."

"Just a little while longer, then I'm going to force you to rest."

Livie placed her pen down beside the ledger and looked at Theo. "Did I tell you that we received a letter from Lady Dianna's family?"

"No," Theo answered, then sat in a chair in front of her desk as if he knew she had more she wanted to tell him.

"They sent a sizable contribution for her upkeep, but they don't want their granddaughter returned to them. They want her to remain here."

"And you're telling me this because…?"

"I've named her Kathrine, but am calling her Katie."

"And you're telling me this because…?"

"I am going to raise her. I promised Lady Dianna that I would take care of her baby and I can't do that if I let someone else adopt her."

Livie watched Theo relax in his chair. He crossed his arms across his chest and stretched his long, muscular legs out in front of him. She studied his expression, trying to determine if her news upset him.

"Are you angry?"

"Do I appear angry?"

"No," Livie answered.

"I'm not. Your news doesn't surprise me in the least. In fact, if I'm surprised about anything, it's that you *haven't* brought more children under your wing. I have a feeling you'd adopt them all if you could."

Livie couldn't stop a smile from lifting the corners of her mouth.

"Come on, now," Theo said getting to his feet. "You need to go up and rest."

Livie loved how protective Theo was, but she had to convince him not to be so overprotective. She wasn't used to having someone hover over her like he was doing.

And, they still hadn't talked about Jamie.

Theo knew Jamie was his son, but he hadn't faced her with the fact that he had a son she hadn't told him about. And she hadn't brought up the subject. She knew that was the cause of contention between them. She knew he was angry that she'd kept that from him, but didn't know how to handle the problem yet.

They'd have to talk about it soon though; it was driving a wedge between them that would only become more contentious the longer they didn't talk about it.

"Come with me, then," Theo said taking her hand and looping it through his. "I'll take you to see our son. You can make sure he's all right."

Livie tried to recover from his words. He'd said, *let's go see our son.* That means he knew. He knew Jamie was his.

Livie walked down the hall with him and when they reached Jamie's room, Theo opened the door and followed her in.

"Mama!" Jamie greeted and ran toward her and wrapped his arms around her. He wasn't tall enough to reach Livie's back, so Theo let them embrace.

"Are you all better, now?"

"Almost, Jamie. Much better than the first time you saw me."

"Yah, you were hurt really bad."

"Yes, I was."

"Do you need Ralphie to stay with you again? I can give him back."

"No, Jamie. He can stay with you. I don't need him any-more."

"I'm glad," Jamie said, hugging his bear to his chest. "I missed him when you had him."

"I know you did. That's why I didn't keep him any longer. But I don't need him anymore."

Livie and Jamie talked a few more minutes, then she rose and gave her son a kiss on the cheek and told him good bye. Then, she and Theo left Jamie's room.

"Would you mind if we stopped at my room?"

"Of course not."

"I just need to sit for a few moments."

"Of course."

Theo took her to her room and helped her sit behind her desk. *I need to talk to you, Theo.* She wanted to talk to him about Jamie. She wanted him to know everything about his son and what she'd gone through when she discovered that she was pregnant. And, she wanted to tell him that she wasn't sure why, but there was something about McBride that bothered her. She wasn't sure what it was, but she didn't trust him.

Livie was about to bring up the subject of Jamie when there was a knock on the door and Commander McBride entered with Jack behind him.

Livie stared at the commander. There was something Agent Wallace had said before he died.

Why couldn't she remember what it was? She'd asked him what McBride had looked like so she could recognize him and he said, *he has a… scar on his… forehead. He has a… scar on his… forehead.*

Livie's gaze darted to McBride's forehead and her breath caught. She clamped her hands together until her fingers ached.

There was no scar on his forehead. He wasn't who he said he

was. He was impersonating the real McBride to get the papers and the jewel.

Livie locked her gaze with Theo's. She had to let him know that the man with them wasn't McBride, but when she turned back to watch McBride, her breath caught.

With a slow, deliberate move, his hand went to the pistol at his waist. He was letting her know that he would use it if she threatened to expose him and someone would die. Most likely Theo. She couldn't let that happen.

Jack went to the window and looked out. "We have a problem," he said to Theo.

"What is it?"

"Several more French troops have just joined the French army."

Theo rose to his feet. "How many?"

"Enough that we won't be able to fight them off if they attack," McBride answered.

"Why?" Livie asked. "Why now?"

"They're convinced that you have the papers and the jewel and they want them back. They've been watching and they know we haven't sent a patrol to take what Wallace stole from them to London."

"Or," Livie said, "the traitor told the French that we still have the papers and jewel here." Livie's gaze locked with Theo's. "They're going to attack us, Theo."

"No doubt," Theo answered, pulling back the curtains at the window. "But not anymore today. Soldiers are still arriving and it will be dark before they're all here. That will give us time to prepare for an attack," Theo answered.

Livie rose from behind her desk. "No, Theo. What about the children? We won't be able to keep them safe."

Before Theo could respond, the door opened and a stranger entered the room.

"Quinn!" Theo and Jack said in greeting. "How did you get here?"

"I had to sneak in by a back way. I came to warn you. Waterford was ordered to take his men back to London."

"He what?" Commander McBride said in a voice filled with fake anger.

"He received orders this morning to break camp and return to London."

"Who issued the order?" Jack asked.

"All he said was that his troops weren't needed here and would be better served in London."

"I guess that proves who our traitor is," McBride said.

"Does it?" Livie asked in an accusing tone. She wanted McBride to know she didn't trust him She wanted him to know she knew he was the traitor.

"Of course it does," McBride countered.

"You seem quick to cast blame on Commander Waterford," Livie said. "Why is that, Commander?"

"How dare you," McBride said taking an angry step toward her.

"Stop right there, Commander," Theo said stepping between Livie and Commander McBride.

A chasm of silence separated the people in the room. Hostile glances clashed between Livie and Commander McBride and neither of them seemed ready to back down.

"I was with Waterford when he received the order," Quinn said. "He wasn't at all pleased with his orders. He even considered disobeying them."

"What are we going to do, Commander?" Theo asked.

Commander McBride finished the liquor in his glass. "Mrs. Matthews is going to hand over the papers and the jewel. Right now!"

Chapter Thirteen

Theo stopped the heated conversation from becoming more hostile, and took Livie from the room, explaining that she'd been up too long and wasn't thinking clearly. But Livie's mind had never been clearer in her life.

Instead of letting Theo take her back to her office, she took him down the stairs, then led him out a side door and down the middle path in the small flower garden on the side of the orphanage.

"What were you doing back there, Livie? Trying to get yourself arrested?"

Livie looked at Theo and recognized the anger in his glare. She knew he didn't understand why she'd battled with Commander McBride but she'd wanted to see how he reacted when she pushed him. And she found out. He became more desperate for her to hand over the papers and the jewel. Except, Livie didn't think McBride cared one bit about the papers. He only wanted the jewel.

"Do you remember when you told me to keep the papers and the jewel from McBride?"

Theo raked his fingers through his hair. That was a habit of his when he was frustrated. Or confused.

"I don't know, Livie. I just…"

"You just don't trust him," Livie finished for him. "That's

why you didn't want me to give the papers and the jewel to him."

Theo sat on the cement bench and looked out on some flowers that hadn't bloomed yet. "Maybe. I don't know. Something's not right. I just can't put my finger on it."

"I can, Theo. What if McBride – or whoever he is – is the traitor?"

"What?"

"What if McBride is the traitor?"

"No, Livie. He can't be. He outranks Waterford."

"That doesn't mean anything, Theo. He can still be the traitor."

"You have to be mistaken, Livie," Theo said.

Theo looked at her, then took her in his arms and held her.

He didn't believe her. He didn't believe that McBride was the traitor. Nor did he believe that the man claiming to be McBride was an imposter. He thought she was imagining it. But she wasn't.

"What happens if McBride gets the jewel, Theo?"

"He'll turn it over to the British."

"What if he doesn't? What if he sells it to the French?"

"He'll become a very wealthy man."

"What will happen if McBride can't get the jewel for the French, Theo? What if I refuse to give it to him?"

Theo didn't answer immediately. Finally, he answered in a softer, more pensive voice. "I'm not sure, Livie."

"But you have an idea, don't you?"

Theo couldn't meet her gaze. Instead, he focused on a place in the garden.

"If I don't give the French the papers and the jewel, they are going to come after them, aren't they?"

"More than likely," Theo answered. "But don't worry. We're not alone. We still have the twenty soldiers McBride brought with him."

"Compared to what, Theo? Three times that many French soldiers. Four? And how do we know we can trust McBride's soldiers? McBride could have hired them to fight us for the papers and the jewel."

"Come here, Livie." Being careful of her back, Theo wrapped his arm around her and led her to the nearest bench in the area where the children often played.

Livie nestled her head beneath Theo's chin and listened to his heart beat beneath her ear. He was frightened. Even though he didn't show how afraid he was, his rapid heartbeat told her he wasn't as calm as he pretended to be.

"What are we going to do, Theo? How are we going to stop the French from attacking?"

"We may not be able to," he answered on a sigh. "We may have to fight them. That may be our only course of action."

"No! It can't be, Theo. The chance of everyone making it out alive is non-existent. The chance of the children escaping unharmed isn't likely to happen. There has to be another way."

"You're right, Livie. There has to be another way. I just can't see it yet, but I will."

"Maybe we should give them what they want, Theo. Maybe we should hand over the papers and the jewel."

Theo shook his head. "McBride will never allow that to happen. He'll do whatever he has to do to prevent us from giving what Wallace took back from the French."

"Why are they so important, Theo? What do the papers contain?"

"They contain France's battle plans. Their battle plans, should they attack our troops."

"Oh," Livie whispered. "Then they are indeed important to us."

"Yes. They are very important."

"What about the jewel?"

"The jewel is more important to France than to us. France's coffers are empty because of the last war they fought. They need the money from the sale of the jewel to refill their war chests. Otherwise, they are at a distinct disadvantage and won't have enough in reserve to buy weapons and ammunition to arm their men. Or feed and clothe them adequately on the battlefield. This makes France extremely vulnerable, and open to attack from any hostile nation."

"So they need the jewel much more than the papers, and we need the papers more than the jewel."

"In a nutshell, Livie, yes."

"That's our answer then, Theo."

A frown of confusion etched across Theo's forehead. "What is?"

"The jewel is the answer to how we're going to survive this."

"What do you mean, Livie? What are you planning?"

Livie saw the questioning hesitation in Theo's eyes. He didn't trust her. He doubted her allegation that McBride was the traitor and if she continued to accuse him, Theo would only become more convinced she needed to be watched. She couldn't allow that.

"Livie?" he questioned again.

"It's nothing, Theo. I was just thinking."

"Thinking what?" Theo asked with a frown on his face.

"Nothing, Theo. I just realized how serious our predicament was and I'm afraid there may not be a way out of it without losing several lives."

"Don't worry, Livie," he said placing his arm around her. "We'll manage. Jack, Quinn, and I are worth ten of their soldiers, and surely some of the men McBride brought with him are loyal to the Crown."

"I know," Livie said, trying to sound reassured. But in truth, she felt far from it. She had plans to make. She had to find her own way out of this.

"I think I'd like to go in now, Theo. It's been a long day."

"Of course, Livie."

Theo took her hands and held them, then pulled her to him. "We still need to talk, Livie. I want to know what happened to you when you realized you were pregnant, and I wasn't there to stand by you."

Livie lowered her gaze. She preferred to forget that time in her life. It wasn't a time she wanted to remember or talk about.

With a gentle touch, Theo placed his finger beneath her chin and tilted her head upward. When his gaze was locked with hers, he lowered his head until his mouth covered hers.

Livie wasn't sure she was ready for Theo's kisses, and yet, there was nothing she wanted more. She had never been able to deny his kisses. Never been able to resist him. Or to give herself to him. The pull he had on her was too strong to deny.

She'd felt it the first time she'd met him. The first time he'd kissed her. There was something magical in the way they were attracted to each other. It was as if they were two parts of the same heart, and soul, and mind. Two parts of the same person.

Theo deepened his kiss and gave her more of himself. The depth of his passion was incredible. It demanded more from her than he'd ever asked of her before.

Livie skimmed her hands up Theo's muscular chest, then wrapped her arms around his neck and held him securely. She refused to let him go. She needed him too much. She loved him too completely. She didn't ever want to lose him. Not in this lifetime or the next.

Livie threaded her fingers through Theo's hair and cupped his head. He deepened his kiss and she firmed the pressure of his mouth against hers. She couldn't get enough of his passion. She couldn't show him how desperate she was to return his demands.

There was nothing she wouldn't give him. Nothing she would deny him.

Suddenly, she had an answer to their problem. She knew what she had to do. Even if Theo hated her for it. Even if he considered it a traitorous act. Even if he could not protect her from the consequences.

Theo kissed her again, then broke off their kiss and pulled her to him. He held her tight and nestled her close. "I love you, Livie. I always have."

"I know, Theo. Even when you weren't there with me I knew you loved me. We were made to be together."

He kissed her once more, then wrapped her in his arms and took her back to the orphanage. "You need to rest. You've been up far too long today. You're dead on your feet."

He led her to her room, then kissed her once more. "Livie, promise me you won't do anything foolish. Promise me you'll let Jack, Quinn, and me handle this."

"Of course, Theo. Who better than you and your friends to protect us?"

"Don't worry, Livie. We'll take care of you. And the children."

"I know, Theo. I know."

And she watched him leave.

Livie's eyes filled with tears that spilled over her lashes and ran down her cheeks.

Theo may think he could protect her and the children, but he couldn't. There were too many French soldiers to stand up against. If the French attacked, not everyone would survive. And Livie knew she could not survive if Theo was killed. Not after she'd just found him again.

She knew what she had to do. She had to avoid a battle if at all possible. She had to avoid any harm coming to the children. Even if Theo hated her for what she was about to do.

And she knew he would.

LIVIE STAYED AWAKE until the orphanage was mostly quiet. With more than twenty babies and children, The Angel's Wings was never totally quiet, but tonight that would work in her favor.

She stayed in her room and considered the repercussions that would occur after Commander McBride and the other officers realized what she'd done. Commander McBride would be furious, as would Jack and Quinn. But she could live with their fury. Theo's fury was another matter.

He would be angry with her for several reasons, all of them justified. But she had no choice. She could not let any of the men die. She could not risk harm coming to any of the children. Or the young lasses who were here until they had their babes. And she could never live with herself if something happened to Theo because she hadn't done all she could to protect him.

She knew she had no choice. She had to do everything in her power to keep everyone safe. Possession of a jewel wasn't worth anyone's life. She hoped she could live with Theo's anger when it was over. She hoped, perhaps, in time he would understand why she did what she had. Even if he could not forgive her.

When she was sure Theo and the other soldiers were asleep, she crept from her room and made her way to Jamie's bedside. She knew someone would be on patrol. All she had to do was make sure they didn't see her when she left.

When she reached Jamie, she took the bear he always slept with and removed it from his arms. She opened the seam at the bear's neck, removed the jewel she'd hidden there after she'd discovered the dying agent, and put it in her pocket. Then, she went down the back stairway and escaped out the kitchen door.

Livie's heart thundered in her breast. She wasn't sure she was brave enough to return to the French camp after what had happened to her there a short while ago, but what choice did she have?

When she was almost to the camp, she stopped behind a clump of trees and took the jewel from her pocket. She dug a hole in the ground and buried the jewel there, then covered the jewel and continued on her way to the French campsite.

Her heart thundered in her ears with each step she took. Several times she wanted to turn around and go back, but she forced her feet to keep moving forward until she reached the edge of the camp.

Two French soldiers captured her the moment she came

within sight and took her to the commander's tent. They roughly pushed her inside and she stumbled to her knees.

She hadn't realized she was as weak as she was. She thought she was stronger, but evidently she wasn't as healed from the beating she'd received at the Frenchman's hands as she thought. It took all her fortitude to attempt to rise to her feet and face the man who'd caused her so much pain.

"What a surprise, Madam," the commander said when a soldier pulled her to her feet and pushed her in front of the man who'd beat her so severely. He wore a sly grin on his face that caused Livie to consider whether coming here was the wisest move she could have made.

"Did you enjoy your treatment so thoroughly that you returned for more?"

The French commander stepped close to her and lifted her chin until she had no choice but to look him in the eyes.

"No, Commander. It was my hope that I would never have to set eyes on you again, but such was not my good fortune. You are indeed a poor excuse for a man."

The commander's sly grin faded, only to be turned into a taunting glare. Livie tried to tell herself the French officer wouldn't repeat his actions of the past, but she couldn't convince herself that he wouldn't. He enjoyed causing pain entirely too much.

"Why don't you tell me why you were so foolish as to return, Madam?"

Livie took a step back in order to separate herself from the commander. "I know what you want, Commander. You want the papers that are in our possession as well as the jewel. Am I correct?"

The French commander lifted his shoulders in a noncommittal shrug. "Perhaps."

"Then, let me explain what I am willing to offer you."

A malicious grin slowly lifted the corners of his mouth. "You make it sound as if you are the person in charge of this transaction, Madam, when I doubt you possess that much authority."

"That's where you are mistaken, Commander. I am completely in charge because I am the one in possession of the papers as well as the jewel."

His expression changed. His lips tightened and the bitter smile turned stony with anger. "Then I suggest you hand them over right now or you will watch the few soldiers left to protect you die, as well as the children in your care."

"If even one of the soldiers is harmed, or one of the children in my care is hurt, I promise that you will never find the papers or the jewel."

The French commander laughed. "You think you have what we want hidden so well that we will never find them?"

Livie took a step closer to him and stared at him with an unyielding glare. "I know I do. I have them hidden where you will never find them. Not even if you search until you take your dying breath."

The commander sucked in an angry breath and held it.

Livie smiled. "What I know is how much I will enjoy thinking of you returning to France having failed in your mission to recover the papers as well as the jewel. And the ribbing and jesting you will endure when your fellow soldiers discover that you were bested by a woman."

The commander took several steps away from her then stopped and turned back to face her. "You said you had an offer to present. What is it?"

"I have in my possession the papers that were taken from you as well as the jewel. I am willing to return one of the items to you, but not the other. You may have either the papers or the jewel, but not both of them. The choice is yours."

"And in return for the papers or the jewel, what is it you demand?"

"Your agreement that you and your soldiers will be aboard the ships you arrived on and return to France by noon today."

"You cannot be serious," the French commander countered.

"But I am," Livie answered. "Completely serious."

"How do I know I can trust you?"

"I give you my word."

"Which is worth nothing!"

"Plus, I will stay here as your hostage until I am convinced your soldiers are aboard ships and have sailed back to France. When I am assured that your soldiers are gone and the children and everyone else at the orphanage is safe, I will give you what you want."

A gleeful expression changed the commander's features. "Does your commander know the offer you are making?"

"No. I am the one who possesses the papers and the jewel, therefore I will decide what is done with them."

The commander dropped his head back on his shoulders and laughed. "Then I offer you this word of warning. Prepare yourself for what will come when the commander and the other officers with him discover what you've done."

"I already know what will probably happen. You see, I know that Commander McBride is a spy and a traitor, as well as a murderer, and so does Captain Dunworthy. By the time Captain Dunworthy realizes I am gone, Commander McBride will probably be arrested, along with the soldiers he brought with him."

The French Commander stared at her with a narrowed glare. "You have made yourself a very powerful enemy, my lady. I fear you will live to regret it."

"That is not your problem, Commander. All you need to do is tell me what you want, the papers or the jewel, and make sure your men are aboard the ships by noon and have returned to France."

"The jewel," the commander answered without hesitation. "Of course, I want the jewel."

"I assumed you would want the jewel, so I brought it with me."

You knew that is what I would want?"

"That is the only object that has value to you."

"You are not just a pretty face, are you Madam?"

"No, Commander. I've never considered myself to have a pretty face. But I've always known I had a keen mind."

"Very well, Madam. We have a bargain. There are several ships waiting offshore. My men will be on them and on their way to France by noon. When you are sure I've kept my part of the bargain, you will give me the jewel and I will leave with it."

"And I will never see you again."

The commander smiled. "If that is your wish."

"That is most definitely my wish."

"As you desire," he said, then turned to the soldiers keeping guard and ordered them to wake the soldiers and have them break camp. When he finished, he turned to face her. "Please, make yourself comfortable, Mrs. Matthews. You will be my guest for the next several hours."

Livie turned and watched the commander leave the tent, then sat behind his small desk and thought about what would happen when Theo realized she was gone.

But that was nothing when compared to how McBride would react when he realized what she'd done. He would look on her actions as treasonous. And so would Theo. And there would be nothing Theo could do to help her.

The soldier in him no doubt thought that he and Jack and Quinn had the skill to defeat the entire French army by themselves, but Livie knew that was impossible without at least one of them dying in the battle. And what if some of those injured or dead were the children? Perhaps even Jamie. Livie couldn't let that happen. She couldn't live with herself if something happened to Jamie.

No, her biggest threat was Commander McBride. She didn't know what his real name was, but one fact she was sure of, he was part of Her Majesty's Army and he had enough rank that he could bring her up on charges if he chose to. And he would definitely choose to do everything he could to punish her if she spoiled his chances of becoming a very wealthy man.

She considered what all would happen before this day was over.

She'd done what she had to do to save Theo.

She'd done what was necessary to make sure nothing happened to Jamie or any of the other children.

And, she'd exposed the traitor in Her Majesty's Army.

Except, what she'd done had forced her to lose the man she loved. The man who possessed her heart.

CHAPTER FOURTEEN

THEO SAT AROUND the table with Commander McBride, Jack, Quinn, and three of McBride's strategists. Their main topic of concern was how to ward off an attack from the French.

McBride, Jack, and Quinn were convinced that Commander Waterford was the traitor. He had to be the one working with the French. Who else would have given them England's battle plans? Why he had turned against England was still a mystery, but he had. He was also the traitor who'd informed the French that Frank Wallace had taken the battle plans and the jewel.

Which made him the one responsible for Frank Wallace's death.

Theo, however, had his doubts. And out of respect and friendship for Theo, Quinn and Jack held their opinions.

Waterford had been Theo's commander for years. Theo thought he knew him as well as he knew anyone. He admired him both off and on the battlefield. He couldn't believe anything could make a man like Waterford turn against the country he'd served his entire life.

"How many troops do you estimate the French have, Captain Dunworthy?" McBride asked as he studied a map of their surroundings.

"My guess would be upwards of one hundred and fifty, Commander."

"Those odds aren't the most encouraging," McBride said, pushing himself from his chair and pacing the room. "Any suggestions on how we can make it out of this alive?" McBride paced the room again.

"Not without handing over the papers and the jewel," Jack said.

"Which I refuse to do." McBride raked his hand down his face.

"Even if it was the only way we could save the children and our men?" Theo asked.

"Perhaps it might be worth considering," Quinn suggested in support for Theo's alternative. "For the children's sake."

"No," McBride answered in a firm voice.

Before he could listen to any more suggestions, one of his men entered the room. "Commander, there's significant movement at the French camp."

"What kind of movement, Sergeant?"

"It looks like they are either preparing to attack, or they're tearing down and preparing to leave."

"What?"

"There's a flurry of activity that indicates they are on the move."

A knot formed in Theo's gut and everything inside him told him to get to Livie. He had to protect her and the children.

"I have to take care of the children," Theo said rushing to leave the room.

"Saddle our horses, Sergeant. Colonel Beckham, you stay here and keep guard. Washburn and I will see what's going on."

Everyone ran to their assignments.

"Livie," Theo cried out as he raced up the stairs. She should be in her room resting. She wasn't near healed yet and should be in bed. Besides, he hadn't seen her downstairs.

"Livie!" he cried out again, but again there was no answer.

He reached her room and threw open the door. The room was empty. "Marie! Marie!"

"Yes, Captain."

"Where's Mrs. Matthews? The French are moving. Where's Livie?"

"I don't know, Captain. I haven't seen her all morning. She wasn't here when I rose."

"What do you mean she wasn't here? She has to be here. She's not well enough to leave the orphanage."

"I know, Captain, but I'm afraid she did. Her bed wasn't slept in last night."

Theo looked at the untouched bed and realized Livie hadn't slept in it all night. "Bloody Hell!" he bellowed, then ran from the room and down the stairs. "Quinn! She's gone. Livie's gone."

"Where'd she go?" Quinn asked when Theo rushed into the room.

"I'm afraid she went to the French camp. I think she offered to give them the jewel."

"Why do you think that?"

"Because she asked me which one they would more than likely want. I told her the jewel because it was more valuable and if they found the right buyer, they'd have enough money to fill their war chests."

"Bloody Hell, Theo. Do you know what might be happening to her if she went to bargain with the French?"

"Of course I do. I saw the bastard's handiwork the last time he had her."

Theo and Quinn ran to the stable and saddled their horses. Then, they raced to the French camp. They got there shortly after the commander and Jack.

The camp was deserted. The tents were down, the camp fires extinguished, the horses gone, and there wasn't a sign of anyone except for Livie standing at the edge of the campsite, looking out on the water.

Theo dismounted and walked to where she stood.

"They're gone, Theo. They left."

"What did you do, Livie?"

"I offered the French commander something he couldn't refuse."

Theo squeezed his eyes shut and clenched his hands into fists. He was angrier than he'd ever been in his life. He was filled with enough fury to tear a dozen men apart with his bare hands. And yet… how could he blame her? How could he question her for doing the only thing she could to protect the children? And him?

"Do you realize what you've done, Livie? You could be brought up on charges. You could be charged with treason."

Livie didn't react. She stood still and watched the boats sail further across the channel until they were gone.

"I know you're angry, Theo. And I don't blame you. But I didn't have a choice. It was the only way to protect you and the children and I knew you would never do it."

"No, I could never do it. A man died to get those papers and that jewel. He died because he took the jewel out from under the Frenchmen's noses, and you threw his life away like it was worth nothing."

"His life wasn't worth nothing. It saved the lives of all the children and the babies in the orphanage. His life was worth dozens of human souls. He died to save them. Each and every one of them. And if I had it to do over again, I would do the same thing again."

"Do you know what might happen to you? You could be brought up on charges. McBride could charge you with treason."

"No, he can't."

"What makes you think that?"

"It doesn't matter," Livie answered. "You wouldn't believe me if I told you."

"How can you say that?"

"I can say that because it's true. Just know that I know exactly what I've done. What any parent would have done. I saved our son."

And she turned and walked away from him.

Theo watched her walk past McBride and Jack and Quinn, to

return to the orphanage. He wanted to go after her. She was dead on her feet. It was obvious from her pale complexion and the fact that she could barely lift her feet when she walked. She hadn't slept at all the night before and her lack of sleep had taken a toll. And yet, he couldn't go after her. He was too angry yet. He was terrified that McBride would charge her with treason, and if he did, there was nothing Theo could do to save her.

Theo watched her until she was almost out of sight. Just when she reached the edge of the tree line, she stumbled and went down.

"Bloody hell!" he bellowed and ran after her. "Livie," he said when he reached her. He knelt beside her and lifted her into his arms.

"Jack, get my horse."

Jack ran for his horse and Theo brushed Livie's hair from her face and lifted her in his arms.

"What did she do to make the French leave, Captain," McBride asked in an angry voice.

"She made them choose between the papers and the jewel. They chose the jewel and returned to France with it."

"No!" McBride bellowed. "No! She's committed treason!"

Jack came with Theo's horse before McBride could say more. Jack helped Theo mount with Livie in his arms, and they returned to the orphanage.

Theo carried Livie up the stairs and to her room, then laid her on the bed. "Livie," he whispered as he tried to wake her, but it took much longer than he thought it would.

"Theo?"

"Yes. Don't move, Livie. You need to rest."

He poured some water into a glass and let her drink, then he put some wine in a glass and added a generous dose of laudanum to it before he forced her to drink that, too.

"I'm fine. You don't need to take care of me."

"I don't think you're fine. I think you've gone two days without any sleep and very little food. You were exhausted before you pulled this stunt and staying awake all night didn't help."

"I know you're angry with me."

"I'm not angry, Livie. I'm furious. Do you have any idea what you've done?"

Livie didn't open her eyes. She took in a deep breath and released it slowly. "Yes. I know."

"How am I going to get you out of this mess?"

"You're not. That's why I didn't ask you to help me, or tell you what I was going to do. I didn't want you involved. I knew it would be better this way."

"Oh, sweetheart," he whispered, then leaned down and kissed her on the forehead. "Finish your wine. You need to sleep, and I need to speak to McBride. Maybe he'll see reason."

"No, he won't. He won't see reason. He's too angry. But it doesn't matter, Theo. You and Jamie are safe. That's all that matters."

"But you're not."

"But you are."

Livie finished her wine, welcoming the effects of the laudanum. She just wanted to sleep until this nightmare was over.

THEO PACED FROM one side of Livie's study to the other while he waited for McBride to join him. He didn't have a good feeling about this. Wallace and McBride had been partners. There was nothing more bonding than soldiers who served together and watched each other's back. McBride had taken Wallace's death hard. Theo didn't doubt that he wouldn't take Livie's theft of the items Wallace had given his life to take from the French any better.

Theo poured himself a glass of brandy and took a swallow. He had a feeling he'd need more than just a swallow or two before his discussion with McBride reached a conclusion, especially when his commanding officer accused Livie of several crimes she'd committed, including treason.

He took another drink from his glass and set it down on the table when he heard McBride's heavy footsteps nearing the room. Theo turned when McBride arrived.

"Pour me one of those, too," he said, then sat in Livie's chair behind the desk.

Theo poured his commanding officer a glass of brandy and handed it to him, then stood in front of the desk. The deep furrows across McBride's forehead indicated an anger that caused Theo's nerves to rise. His fury was palpable. He clenched his jaw and the harsh breaths he took hissed through his teeth.

"I'd tell you to sit down, Dunworthy, but it won't take long to get this over. A crime as obvious as this doesn't leave much room for discussion."

Theo didn't relax but stood with his muscles taut and his shoulders locked.

McBride took a swallow of his brandy then slammed his glass on the desk. "Explain why the hell she did it."

"Because she knew it was the only solution to the French's desperation sir. The jewel is more valuable than simply what it's worth in a monetary sense of the word. It holds a significant historic value as well. The French commander would have lost all credibility if he had returned to France without it."

"Wasn't Mrs. Matthews aware that her actions would be considered treasonous?"

Theo closed his eyes and squeezed them tight. "Yes. I have no doubt she was."

"Yet she acted on her decision anyway."

"Yes, Sir."

"Why?" McBride bellowed. "Didn't she realize how desperate we were to have the jewel to bargain with? Didn't she realize how valuable it was? And yet she gave it away as if it was hers to do with what she wanted. Why?"

"Because she is one of the most remarkable caregivers you

will ever meet. She holds each and every one of the children, from the newborn babes to the oldest children here, in the highest regard. She loves each and every one of them and will do anything in her power to protect them."

"Including committing treason to protect them."

"Yes," Theo answered. "Livie was convinced that the French were so desperate to recover the jewel they would attack the orphanage and everyone in it to retrieve the jewel. Just as she was convinced that if they attacked, the probability was extremely high that some of the children, as well as many of us who are here to protect the children, would not survive the attack."

"They are only children, Dunworthy! Children who belong to no one and who no one wants. They are nothing compared to the amount of riches possession of the jewel will provide."

Theo was shocked by McBride's words but tried not to show it. "I'm not sure that is fair, sir."

"You're not? What about our negotiators losing the bargaining power that possession of the jewel gave us. Do you think that is fair?"

Theo knew better than to respond. McBride was too angry to see reason. The less Theo said the better.

"So what do you suggest I do about what Mrs. Matthews did?"

"I'm afraid I'm not the right person to ask, Sir."

"Why is that, Captain?"

"Because I love her, Sir. We share a past, and a son. I would gladly assume the punishment in her place rather than see her accused of treason. The lady already proved her loyalty and her love of country when she endured being whipped rather than hand over the papers and the jewel. Her previous actions prove she is not a traitor."

"The lady proved nothing, Captain! Except she was willing to steal a jewel that didn't belong to her and commit treason."

McBride slid the chair back from the desk and stood. "One more thing, Captain. I would like to speak with Mrs. Matthews alone for one second. Is she in her room?"

"Yes, sir. But she has had a difficult day."

"We have all had a difficult day, Captain. A *very* difficult day."

"Yes, sir. If you'll follow me," Theo said, then led the way to Livie's room. Theo opened the door and the commander stopped him from entering. "I want to speak with Mrs. Matthews alone," he said, then closed the door behind him.

"Mrs. Matthews," he called out. "Mrs. Matthews," he repeated louder. Angrier.

⟶⟫⟩⟨⟪⟵

LIVIE OPENED HER eyes and looked at him. The man who had the ability to arrest her glared down at her. "Commander McBride," she whispered.

"I understand that you spoke to the French commander."

Livie tried to focus on Commander McBride but she had such a difficult time waking that it was impossible.

She struggled to keep her eyes open. She'd seen him briefly before but hadn't had the opportunity to study him. Now she did. This was the man Agent Wallace told her would be coming to get the papers and the jewel. This was the man called Jason. The man with the—

Livie tried to study his facial features. This was the man Wallace said had a scar on his forehead. But there was no scar on McBride's forehead.

"Who are you?" she asked.

"Commander McBride, Mrs. Matthews. Commander Jason McBride."

Livie shook her head. "No, you're not. You don't have a scar," she said. "You're supposed to have a scar. He said you'd have a scar."

Commander McBride leaned closer and clamped his fingers around her arm. He was hurting her and Livie knew he intended to.

Suddenly, she was frightened. She looked around for Theo but he wasn't there. "Where's Theo? What have you done to him?"

"If I were you, I'd be more worried about yourself than the captain."

"Waterford isn't the traitor. You are."

"Those are dangerous accusations, Mrs. Matthews. They could get you killed."

"If anything happens to me, Theo will know you're responsible. He'll figure out that you're the traitor."

"It's unfortunate that you know that, Mrs. Matthews. Very unfortunate indeed. And telling me was very foolish. Now, I'm afraid you will have to pay for your foolishness," he said as he squeezed her arm harder. "I'm afraid now I will have to kill you. Not today. Not now. But soon. When you least expect it."

Livie blinked, then shook her head to clear it. Surely she hadn't heard him correctly. Surely he hadn't just threatened to kill her.

She opened her eyes to find him.

But he was gone.

McBride's threat remained engrained in her mind. A cold chill raced down her spine and a shiver shook her. His words echoed in her head.

She could pray she'd imagined it.

But knew she hadn't.

✦

CHAPTER FIFTEEN

LIVIE OPENED HER eyes and her gaze locked with Theo's broad shoulders and long, muscular legs stretched out before him. His arms were crossed in a relaxed pose, and his chin rested on his chest.

Livie didn't know how long she'd been asleep, but somehow she knew Theo had been with her the entire time.

"Theo," she whispered softly. "Theo."

His eyes opened and he sat up. "Are you awake?"

"Yes. How long have I been asleep?"

"Several hours."

"You shouldn't have let me sleep so long."

"I had to. Marie and the rest of the staff would have had my head if I had awakened you. They're quite protective of you."

Livie couldn't help but smile. "They always have been."

"I can see that." Theo reached for her hand and held it. "How do you feel?"

"I'm fine. A little tired yet, but fine."

"Do you still hurt?"

"No. I don't need anything. I'm fine. Where's McBride?" she asked.

"He's gone."

"Where?"

"He went to London. He said there was no reason for him to

stay now that the French were gone."

"Theo, there's something you need to know."

Livie looked at the expression on Theo's face and the words wouldn't come. Whatever it was she wanted to say was trapped inside her mind and wouldn't come out. But whatever it was could stay there. McBride was gone now and there was no reason for him to come back. They were too far away from London and too far from anyone in authority who could prosecute him.

"What is it, Livie?" Theo asked.

"Nothing, Theo. It's nothing. Did you talk to McBride before he left?"

"No."

"Did he say what he was going to do?"

"No. I don't think he's made up his mind."

"It doesn't matter. He can't arrest me."

"How can you say that?"

"Because it's true. He doesn't have the power to arrest me for treason."

Livie sat up and dangled her feet over the bed. "I need to see Jamie."

"Jamie's fine. He's in the nursery with the rest of the children."

"Theo, if McBride comes after me, take Jamie and get him away from me."

"No, Livie. Don't say it. Don't think it. Nothing is going to happen to you."

"But you know it's possible that McBride *will* come after me. And if he does, promise me you'll take care of Jamie. Promise me you won't let him grow up alone."

"He'll never be alone, Livie. I'll never let him grow up alone. He'll have a family. You, me, and maybe even a brother or sister or two."

Livie's eyes filled with tears. That's what she'd dreamed of when she first fell in love with Theo. She'd dreamed of the fairytale life she'd have with him. Until her life turned into anything but a fairytale. Until Theo left her to face her future alone.

"Come, sit with me," he said and led her to the one chair that sat in her sparsely decorated bedroom. Theo sat and pulled Livie onto his lap. She nestled against him and sat with her head beneath his chin.

"I've learned that life doesn't always turn out the way you think it will," she said when she was settled. "That the life you dream of having doesn't always happen like you thought it would."

"That was my fault. That was because I left you."

"Yes, I can't deny that it was. My world fell apart when you left."

"Tell me what happened to you."

"What good will that do? It won't do either of us any good."

"I need to know, Livie. I need to know what happened to you after I abandoned you. I need to know everything you went through."

Livie took in a deep breath and wrapped her arms around Theo's waist. She listened to his heart thunder beneath her ear.

"Tell me. Tell me everything."

At first, Livie couldn't find the words to tell him everything she'd gone through, but after several encouragements, she worked up the nerve to tell him exactly what had happened. "It took me several weeks to believe you'd actually left me. I couldn't find you anywhere. And I searched all over. Then, shortly after I came to terms with the realization that you weren't coming back, I discovered I was with child. I hid it as long as I could, but eventually I had no choice but to tell my parents."

"Oh, Livie. I'm so sorry. What did they do?"

"What do you think? My father was the vicar. He could hardly condone what I'd done. And he didn't want his parishioners to discover that I was carrying a bastard babe. He invented a story that I'd gone away to stay with an ill aunt who'd fallen and needed someone to take care of her." Livie swallowed hard and swiped at the tears that threatened to spill down her cheeks. The terror she'd felt when she realized she was all alone in the world came flooding back. The desolation she'd felt wrapped around her heart like angry claws threatening to stop her heart from beating. "He forced me to leave."

"Where did you go?"

Livie lowered her gaze and stared at her clenched hands in her lap. "There had been a girl from our parish who'd been with child a year or so before me. Father had found her a place to go to have her child. Mama gave me the name of the home for unwed mothers. I went there, but they didn't have room for me. They told me about The Angel's Wings and I came here."

"How did you get here?"

"I walked."

"All that way? Alone?"

Livie saw the guilt in Theo's eyes and written on his face. "Yes. I was already in labor by the time I arrived and nearly lost Jamie."

"And what about you?"

"I didn't care about me, Theo. In fact, I prayed I would die," she said softly. "I didn't know what I would do with no husband to provide for us, and a baby to raise on my own. I thought death was the best way out of my situation."

"Oh, Livie," Theo said, rubbing his hands up and down her arms. "I am so sorry. This is all my fault."

"No, Theo. Making love to me was not your fault alone. I was an eager participant. I wanted what you offered as much as you did. I just didn't stop to consider what the consequences might be."

"You didn't count on the man who got you with child abandoning you."

"No, that never entered my mind," she whispered.

"Then what happened?"

Livie breathed a deep sigh. "I had Jamie and the women taking care of me refused to let me die. Marie was one of the women who helped me birth Jamie. She told me I had to fight to stay alive because my baby needed me. She told me if I abandoned my baby he'd never know that he was conceived out of love. That he'd grow up believing his mother didn't love him enough to fight to stay alive and his father didn't love him enough to know he existed. Once I saw our son, I couldn't let him grow up thinking he wasn't loved. Because I loved him. More than anything on earth."

"Oh, Livie. What did I do to you?" Theo pressed his finger beneath her chin until her lips were angled enough that his mouth could cover them. He lowered his head and kissed her, then deepened his kiss until he'd stolen the air from her body.

"I'm so very sorry, Livie. I don't know how you can even stand to look at me."

"I can because I love you, Theo. I always have."

"As I love you." He kissed her again. "So, what are we going to do now?"

"I think the question is, what are *you* going to do now? This is where I belong, Theo. I could never leave The Angel's Wings. They need me here. The children need me."

"Yes, they do. I can't imagine them getting along without you."

"And I don't want them to have to try."

Livie wrapped her arms around Theo's neck and nestled closer to him. This was where she belonged. In this place. In his arms. But the choice wasn't hers to make. Just as Theo had left her before, he would leave her again. His work with the government was too important to give up to make a life with her at The Angel's Wings. The country needed him too badly for him to walk away from the work he did for them. And it wouldn't be fair of her to ask him to give that work up.

Livie stayed in Theo's arms for several minutes, until a knock on the door interrupted them. Theo and Livie quickly separated.

"Excuse me," a deep, velvety voice said from the doorway. "Am I interrupting you?"

"No, Quinn. Come in."

Theo's fellow special agent entered, then closed the door behind him.

"He's gone," Quinn said. "But I assume you knew that."

"Yes, he went back to London."

Livie turned her head and her gaze locked with Theo's. It was time. She had to tell them. "Something's wrong, Theo."

"What, Livie?"

"Something I should have told you before."

"It's all right, Livie."

"No, it isn't. It's something I should have told you when I first discovered it."

"Why didn't you?" Theo asked.

"I was afraid you wouldn't believe me."

"I would have believed you, Livie. I'd believe anything you told me."

"Not this."

Theo locked his gaze with hers and looked at her with a frown on his face. What is this secret you were afraid I wouldn't believe?"

"It's McBride, Theo. He's the… the traitor."

Theo and Quinn looked at each other. "Bloody hell."

SEVERAL DAYS PASSED, and during that time, Theo let Livie do little more than sleep and sit in her study for a few hours each day. By the time he sent Marie up to tell her that Mrs. Barnes had dinner ready and Livie was finally allowed to leave her room and come down to eat, Livie was ready to climb walls.

"Mrs. Barnes wanted me to bring you and the Captain down. She says you haven't eaten hardly anything in forever and she doesn't want you getting sick again."

"That sounds wonderful," Livie said, sliding off of Theo's lap and walking to the door. Theo and Quinn followed her into the small dining room where Jack was waiting for them.

Food was already on the table and Theo helped her sit, then took the chair beside her. "This looks and smells delicious. I didn't realize how hungry I was," Livie said when they started eating.

"What are you going to do now that the French are gone?" Theo asked his two friends as they ate.

"We've been ordered to stay here with you, in case the French return," Jack said.

"Or in case McBride returns," Quinn added. "We've informed the head office what Livie believes and they're looking into it. Several men in authority believe she is correct. McBride didn't return like he said he would. He's long gone. That doesn't look good."

"You're not the only one who believes that the man pretending to be McBride isn't the real Jason McBride," Jack said.

Livie placed her fork beside her plate and looked at the three men with her at the table. "Have they found the real McBride's body? I assume he's no longer alive."

"No, he's probably not alive, but they haven't found his body yet either," Quinn said.

"Is that why they want you to stay with me? Are they afraid he's going to come back here?" Livie asked.

"There's always that possibility," Jack said.

"Well, whatever their reason," Quinn said, "I'm afraid you'll have to put up with us for at least a little while."

"Can you be gone from your estate right now, Quinn?" Theo asked. "It's well into spring and the crops need to be planted and field work needs to be done."

"My estate will manage, at least for a while."

"Good," Theo finished, "because I have something I'd like to talk to you about. Perhaps after we finish eating."

"Of course," Quinn said, stabbing the potatoes and the meat on his plate.

"And I am completely at your disposal. I don't have anything that needs my attention," Jack said with a grin on his face. "Except, perhaps, making a few lonely London widows exceedingly happy."

Theo and Quinn both laughed at Jack's comment. Theo simply smiled at Livie when she pretended she didn't understand what Jack meant, even though she sniggered behind her napkin. Jack's reputation as a womanizer was well known. Unfortunately, he had the charm and exceeding good looks to make good on that reputation.

The four of them finished their meal, then rose from the table and adjourned to the one and only sitting room in the orphanage. It was the room that they used when interviewing prospective couples looking to adopt one of the children, or a couple bringing their daughter who needed to stay until she had her babe.

"Please, be seated," Livie said, then walked to the cupboard where Theo had stored an assortment of liquor for his friends. Livie poured them each a glass of brandy, which was what Theo and his friends preferred. When she'd given them each a glass and they'd taken a swallow, she sat.

She knew what Theo was going to talk about. It was his plan to ask his friends for advice as well as assistance in helping the orphanage provide for the children.

"What is it, Theo?" Jack asked. "Is something wrong?"

"In a manner of speaking, although not nearly as serious as what we've had to deal with concerning the French. This concerns the children and providing for them."

"What is it?" Quinn asked. "Do you need monetary assistance? If that's it, I'm not a poor man."

"Although the orphanage would never turn down a contribution, that solution is only temporary. Our monetary shortage is ongoing. We need to find a solution that will provide a long-term remedy."

"And you have something in mind that will do just that, don't you, Theo?"

"Yes."

"We should have known," Jack said on a laugh. "You were the one we always went to when there was a problem. You could fix almost any dilemma we came upon. So, what's your plan?"

Theo looked at Livie. "You tell them, Livie."

"Well," she began, "I do the accounts for the orphanage and while the number of children needing food and clothing and care is continually increasing, there continues to be a shortage of money to purchase what we need. Theo was aware of how desperate our condition was, and one day he came to me with an idea. He had been thinning out a thicket of raspberry, blackberry, and gooseberry bushes and commented that if all the bushes produced fruit, we'd have an overabundance of fruit at our disposal. That's when he came up with the idea that we could make use of the fruit from the bushes to make jams and jellies, and set up a little shop in London to sell our products."

"That's a fantastic idea," Quinn said. "You can rely on me to provide the start-up costs. It will take some kind of investment to purchase jars to fill with the jams and jellies."

"Yes," Livie added. "And sugar to make the product."

"And Frank tells me there is a very productive strawberry patch and some blueberries on the other side of the hedgerow where the raspberries are."

"That is amazing. You'll have a never-ending supply of fruit," Quinn said. "And I saw some orange trees. They can be used for orange marmalade."

Livie smiled. There's no limit to the jams and jellies we can sell in our little shop."

"With supervision, the older children can be relied on to man the shop," Theo added.

"And we could set aside one day a week to ask for volunteers from the village and the church to help make the jams and jellies right here at the orphanage," Livie said.

"And the children can devote an hour every day in season to picking the berries," Theo added. "We should have our business up and running in no time."

"That's a brilliant idea," Jack said, then topped everyone's glass. "Have the berries ripened yet?"

"Nearly," Theo said. "They should be ready to pick by the end of the week."

"That should give us time to get everything ready," Livie said. "We'll have to order jars from the shoppe in the village, and sugar. And organize a crew to start making the jams and jellies next week."

"And we'll need to make a trip to London to find an empty place to sell our product," Quinn said.

"And make the rounds of all the eating establishments and stores that sell food products and leave them samples to try and then to sell," Jack said.

"Oh, my," Theo said on a sigh. "I had no idea there was so much involved in setting up a business. It's a good thing Livie has a sharp head on her shoulders for the business end of things."

"I'll go to the village tomorrow and order jars and purchase sugar, and anything else we'll need," Theo said.

"And I'll make a list of the women we can ask to help us make the jams and jellies," Livie said. "And I'll ask the vicar to announce after service Sunday that we need volunteers to help us."

"And I'll go to London to scout for a suitable location to set up our shop, and run our business," Quinn said.

"And I'll—" A frown darkened across Jack's forehead. "What should I do?"

"You can stay here and organize a schedule with Marie for a time when the children can start picking the berries," Livie said. "I'll be here to help you as soon as I've talked to the vicar, and visited with enough ladies to get us going."

"Quinn will be the only one who will be gone for any length of time. The rest of us will be here to get things organized," Theo said.

Livie couldn't stop a smile from reaching her eyes. "It's unbelievable how fast this plan has come together. I can't believe that it might be possible for The Angel's Wings to have enough money to feed and clothe the children without having to beg for donations."

"Well, believe it, Livie," Theo said, wrapping his arm around her shoulders and pulling her close to him. "We'll be making a profit before the snow flies."

"Thank you," Livie said to Theo and his friends. "This wouldn't be possible without you."

"We did it for the children," Quinn said. "If anyone knows how much it costs to feed and clothe more than one or two children, it's me. I went from no children just a year ago to having five. Believe me, I understand what an expense children are."

Everyone in the room laughed, but the laughter wasn't only because of Quinn's joke, it was more because of the excitement of their new adventure.

Everything was starting to look more promising. If only their optimism would last.

But, of course, that seldom happened.

✦

CHAPTER SIXTEEN

T HEO WENT TO the village and placed an order for several cases of jars for the jams and jellies, as well as enough sugar to get started on their products, then returned to the orphanage. He found Jack investigating the berry bushes. They were loaded with berries, ready to be picked.

"Are you back already?" Jack asked when he saw Theo coming toward him.

"Yes, it didn't take me long at all to order the supplies we will need."

I'm glad," Jack said. "I have something I want to talk over with you."

"Is something wrong?" Theo asked.

"I'm not sure. I don't want to alarm Livie, but I feel that our traitor is still out there. You know that feeling you get when you think someone's watching you?"

"Yes," Theo answered.

"Well, I've had that feeling all morning."

"Have you seen anyone?"

"No. I went looking, but didn't find anyone."

"Livie knows he's not the real McBride and he can't take the chance that she'll recognize him and turn him in to the authorities."

Theo raked his fingers through his hair. "I know, Jack. I've thought of little else since Livie told us that she thought he wasn't the real McBride. Especially when she thought he was the traitor Wallace warned her about."

"How did Livie recognize him? How did she know he wasn't the real McBride?" Jack asked.

"She said Wallace described him but she couldn't remember what he'd said about him. He said she'd recognize him but she couldn't remember why."

"As soon as Livie can testify to what Wallace said before he died, she'll be in greater danger than ever. If Commander McBride isn't the real commander, he can't afford to let her live."

"Why do you think he's still here?" Theo said in frustration. "If he was wise, he'd just leave the country."

"Revenge, Theo. I think he intended to steal the jewel himself and sell it back to the French, then live the life of a very rich man. Livie ruined his plans. When she gave the jewel back to the French she not only turned our traitor into a very poor man, but he suddenly became wanted by England and France. He'll never be able to live anywhere without watching over his shoulder. That's an awful lot to hate Livie for."

"Yes, it is. I imagine seeing all that wealth slip through your fingers would make anyone a bitter man who wants revenge."

"And, as long as Livie's alive to recognize him," Jack said, "he'll always be a wanted man.

"In other words, she won't be safe until he's been arrested or he's dead." Theo tried to ignore the pain in his gut but it wouldn't go away. He was going to have to guard Livie night and day until McBride was arrested, or dead.

"That's right," Jack said, then picked a blackberry and ate it. "Don't worry, Theo, nothing will happen to her. We'll make sure she stays safe."

Just then, Livie came toward them. "Don't tell me you're eating all our profits, Major Washburn," she teased.

Jack and Theo laughed with her.

"Did you have any problems getting the jars, Theo?"

"None. They'll be here next Friday. Jack and I can go into town for the sugar later on this week."

"Wonderful. The ladies can come to make our first batch of jam as soon as the jars come in."

"We'd better begin picking, then," Theo said. "We don't want to run short of berries."

"I don't think there's a chance of that happening," Livie said, scanning the long row of berry bushes hanging heavy with fruit. "I can't believe this is going to become a reality. The orphanage will finally become self-supporting."

"Won't that be remarkable? What you've always hoped would happen," Theo said, placing his arm around Livie's shoulder and bringing her close to him. "When do you think our first batch of jams and jellies will be ready to sell, Livie?" Theo asked.

"By the end of the month I would think. We want to have enough of a supply that we don't run out as soon as we get started."

"Don't worry, we won't," Jack said, picking another blackberry and popping it into his mouth.

"We might if you keep eating the berries like you are," Theo teased.

Jack popped one more berry into his mouth, then turned toward the orphanage. "Then we'd better leave here. Besides, I have a few things I need to do before it gets dark."

"What do you have to do?" Livie asked Jack as they made their way back.

"Oh, I want to go for a ride," Jack said. "I haven't ridden Comet for a while and he needs the exercise. Did you want to join me, Theo?"

"No, Jack. I'd rather walk around the grounds."

He and Jack exchanged looks that told each other that it was important that they make sure the grounds were safe and that McBride hadn't returned. Theo could imagine that he'd think this was the most opportune time to move in to attack Livie. Right after the French left and before they could prepare for his attack.

"Would you like to walk with me?" Theo asked Livie? "Or have you had enough exercise for the day?"

"No, I'd love to go for a walk."

"Good."

When they reached the orphanage, Jack went to the stable to saddle his horse, and Theo continued on with Livie. "Do you think Jamie would like to go with us?" Theo asked.

Livie stopped and lifted her head until her eyes were locked with his. "He would love to," she answered. "I think it's time we told him who you are."

"Are you sure, Livie?"

"Yes, Theo. I want him to know that you're his father and that he has one more person in this world who will love him and always take care of him."

"Oh, Livie."

Theo looked at the tears that pooled in Livie's eyes and lowered his head and kissed her. He loved her. Loved her more than was possible to love the woman who was the mother of his child. Even though he didn't deserve her love, he prayed that she could see how much he regretted leaving her all those years ago, and forcing her to have their son on her own.

"Then," Theo said, lifting his mouth from hers, "I think we need to talk about our future together. Now that I know about Jamie, I want us to be a family. I want to be his father."

"But what about your work for the government? Do you intend to continue with that?"

"That's something we have to figure out together, Livie."

A frown covered Livie's forehead and Theo knew she had reservations. Just like Quinn's wife had reservations. And he knew what those reservations were.

"We will, Theo. We'll decide together what's best for us."

He leaned down and kissed her once more. When he broke their kiss, Livie cupped her hand to his cheek.

"I'll go inside and get Jamie. Wait for us here."

Theo smiled. "I will. I'll always wait for you."

Theo watched Livie go inside, then return with Jamie at her side. When Jamie saw Theo, a smile lit his eyes. Theo couldn't have asked for a more positive reaction.

"Theo," Jamie cried out, then ran toward Theo and jumped into his arms.

"Whoa, Jamie! You're getting so big. Pretty soon I won't be able to catch you."

"Yes, you will, Theo. You're the strongest man in the world."

"You think so?" Theo said, putting him down and mussing his hair.

"How about you and I and your mama go for a walk down to the lake?"

"Yes! Can we go fishing?"

"Not today, Jamie. Maybe later this week."

"Okay, we'll just go sit by the water."

"Yes. Let's sit by the water. There's something I want to talk to you about."

"There is? Is it important?"

"Well, yes. I think it's important. I think you will, too."

"All right, let's go."

Theo watched as Jamie raced ahead of them. When they reached the lake, Jamie was already there.

"I beated you."

"So you did. You beat us."

Theo and Livie sat close to the water's edge and Jamie sat between them.

"What did you want to talk to me about, Theo?"

"Well..." For as prepared as Theo thought he was, he suddenly didn't know how to start this conversation. Thankfully, Livie took over for him.

"Jamie, do you remember when you asked me to tell you who your father was?"

"Yes. And you said you'd tell me about him when I got older. Am I old enough now?"

"Yes, Jamie. I think you are old enough now. I think it's time you found out who your father is."

Jamie looked at Theo with a questioning look on his face. "Are you my da?"

"Yes, Jamie. I'm your da," Theo answered.

"Oh, good. I knew it had to be someone like you."

"How did you know that?" Theo asked.

"Because my mama is real particular about who she likes and who she doesn't like, and she likes you, so I knew it would be someone just like you. And besides, she gets a funny look on her face whenever she looks at you."

"I do not," Livie argued.

"Yes, you do, mama. It's like that look you get when you look at the baby kittens. Like they're so cute."

"I do not look at Theo like he's so cute," Livie countered.

"Yes, you do. Except it's different. It's like you like him a lot."

"That's because I do like him a lot."

"So do I." Jamie turned to face Theo. "I'm glad you're my da, but maybe we shouldn't tell any of the other kids at the orphanage that you're my da."

"Why not?" Livie asked.

"Because they might feel bad. None of them have das."

"That's very thoughtful of you, Jamie," Theo said, mussing his son's hair. "We wouldn't want to hurt their feelings."

"No. They'd feel sad 'cause I got a da and they don't."

Theo lifted his gaze and focused on Livie's tear-filled eyes. Just like her, Theo realized he had a very special son.

THE NEXT COUPLE of weeks went by in a blur. Quinn returned from London with the exciting news that he'd found what he thought was the perfect location for their shop. It wasn't in a fashionable part of London, but in an area where the working class people did their shopping. He thought that would lend itself to more sales from the common folk than if they tried to pretend that they catered to the higher class people.

Livie was excited to see their new place of business, but Theo told her it would be better if she waited until they had a shipment of jams and jellies to take to London to stock the shelves before wasting a trip to the city.

Of course he was correct.

The following week, she took the children out every day to pick berries. They had exactly one week to gather enough berries before the ladies were going to descend on the orphanage and make the jams and jellies. Instead of going to London, Livie rode with Theo to the village to collect the jars and the sugar.

"Do you believe how many jars we have?" she said casting a glance to the back of the wagon. "Do you think we'll sell even half of these?"

"I'm sure we will. As soon as customers taste the jams and jellies," Theo said patting her hand, "we'll sell them faster than you can imagine."

"I hope you're right," Livie said on a sigh.

"Believe me, I am. People in the city don't have berry bushes like we do in the country. This will be a treat for them. And when they find out the profits will go to supporting an orphanage, there will be more profits."

Livie watched Theo turn around again and watch the countryside. It was the sixth or seventh time he'd looked over his shoulder as if he was watching for something or someone. "Are you watching for someone, Theo?"

"What?" he asked turning to face the road ahead of them. "No, of course not."

"You just seem to be watching the countryside behind us very closely."

"I'm just interested in what's going on around us."

"Or perhaps, you're interested in who might be watching us," Livie said.

"That's ridiculous."

She was silent for a few moments, then released a heavy breath. "Are you watching for McBride, Theo? Do you think he might come after me?"

"Not really," Theo answered, "but it never hurts to be careful."

"You aren't a very good liar, Theo."

"I guess I haven't had enough practice," he said, then laughed. "You should be happy about that."

"I am," Livie answered, but her face showed that she was worried. "Tell me, Theo. What makes you think he'll come after me? The jewel is back in France's hands and he cannot get his hands on it. I'm not a threat to him any longer."

"But you are, Livie. You are the only one who heard him admit that he killed Wallace. Not only can you recognize him, but you have ruined his life. You destroyed the only chance he had of living the life of a very rich man. This isn't about anything other than revenge. He wants to harm you because you ruined his chance of having the wealth he dreamed of having."

"Oh, Theo. Will this ever end?"

"Yes, Livie. It will end when we catch him and put him away. Until then, we just have to keep an eye out for him."

Livie reached for his arm and held it close to her. They were home now. Coming up on the orphanage's front door.

"Send the boys out to carry in the jars, Livie. They'll need to take them to the kitchen."

And she did. In a matter of minutes, the jars were in the kitchen along with the sugar, and everything else they'd need for their jams and jellies.

Livie stopped and let her gaze rest on Theo's muscled features. She watched the muscles across his back tighten when he lifted one case after another and stacked them where the boys could reach them. Then, he stopped when he noticed her watching him.

His gaze locked with hers and he smiled a heart-stopping grin that caused her heart to leap in her breast.

With slow, determined steps, he reached her and gathered her in his arms. He couldn't stop the attraction he felt for her. Couldn't prevent his arms from wrapping around her and pulling her close. She was the other half of his beating heart. The part of himself that he couldn't get along without. The part of him that had to be there in order to make him whole. In order to make him alive.

He lowered his head and kissed her, then deepened their kiss until they needed to take a breath. Love like this was more powerful than anything he could imagine. He couldn't imagine living without it.

Or living without Livie.

It was a dream becoming a reality. The huge decision he had to make concerning how he would live his life, and what kind of future he envisioned for himself and Livie, was suddenly not as huge as it had been just a few days ago.

He knew without a doubt that he could not live without her. Nor did he want to spend even one day apart from her. And if he continued working for the Crown, he'd be forced to be apart from her for days on end. He'd never know when he'd be called on an assignment, or how long that assignment would take. That suddenly seemed like too much to ask from him. He had a family now, and a position here at the orphanage where he was wanted and needed.

He'd abandoned Livie once before when she needed him desperately. He refused to abandon her again.

He loved her too much.

CHAPTER SEVENTEEN

"Would you like to take a walk through the garden before we retire?" Theo asked Livie when they were ready to retire for the night. They'd need a good night's sleep. Tomorrow would be a long day. The women would be here early to make the jams and jellies.

"I think I'd rather just go up to bed," Livie said stifling a yawn.

Quinn had already gone up and Jack was taking a final turn around the yard. He said he just wanted to get a little fresh air before he turned in, but Livie knew he wanted to check on any sign of McBride.

They thought she didn't know what they were doing, but she did. They were concerned for her safety. They thought she was in danger, even though she didn't think she was. Livie was certain she was safe as long as she was at the orphanage. Why would McBride risk coming back when he was safe as long as he stayed away? "You go on up to bed, Livie. I'll be up shortly," Theo said. "Tomorrow is going to be a long day."

"Yes, it is," she answered. She turned toward the door then stopped. "Theo?"

"Yes, Livie."

"Would you come up with me?"

He walked closer to her. "Yes, Livie. I'm coming up right

now."

"No. I mean… would you come to bed with me? I don't want to be alone tonight."

His look of surprise was clear. "Are you sure, Livie?" he said, clasping his hands on her arms and pulling her close to him.

"Yes, Theo. I need you. More than I've ever needed you."

Theo brought his mouth down over hers and kissed her. The depth of his passion was clear. He needed her as much as she needed him. He answered her need with a desire that was all-consuming.

He lifted his mouth from hers for just a moment, then deepened his kiss with a passion that consumed them both.

"Come," he said, leading her up the stairs and to his room. He lay her on the bed and came down over her.

It had been five years since she'd lain with him. Five years of nights dreaming about him. And tonight, it seemed as if nothing had changed. Their lovemaking was everything she remembered it being. The love she felt for him was as deep and satisfying as it had always been.

When they were complete and sated, Theo pulled her next to him and wrapped his arms around her. "I love you, Livie. I love you with every depth of my being."

"And I love you. I always have. I always will."

Livie tilted her head and they kissed again, then again. They made love a second time before they fell asleep in each other's arms.

Theo wasn't sure when Livie's nightmare woke him but it was sometime after they'd made love a second time. She thrashed on the bed as if she was trying to escape a demon who was after her.

"What is it, Livie?"

"No," she moaned. "It's him. It's him."

"Who, Livie?"

She pushed his chest to get away from him, then screamed a blood-curdling cry.

"Livie!" Theo grabbed her arms and held her. "Wake up, Livie! Wake up!"

"No! No!" she screamed. "He's here! He's here!"

Theo pulled her to him and held her tight. "Who's here, Livie? Who's here?"

"McBride," she screamed. "But it's not him!"

Her breathing was rapid and rough. She couldn't catch her breath. Couldn't calm herself.

Suddenly the door opened and Jack and Quinn entered the room. Theo threw a cover over her and held her.

"What's wrong?" Jack yelled.

"It's nothing," Theo answered. "Just a bad dream. Wake up, Livie. Look at me."

Livie gasped for breath several times then opened her eyes. "Oh, Theo," she said, then buried her head against him. "He was so real. I really thought he was here."

"You're safe, Livie. You're just having a nightmare, Livie. That's all."

"Wallace told me McBride would have a scar on his forehead but he doesn't. That's how I knew. The fake McBride doesn't have a scar."

"No, he doesn't."

"That's how McBride knows Livie can recognize him," Quinn said.

"He's going to kill me," Livie said in huge gasps. "He told me he was going to."

"When did he tell you that?" Theo asked.

"When he came to see me right before he left."

"He has to get rid of her or he's a dead man and he knows it," Jack said.

Theo shared a serious expression with his friends and held Livie tighter.

"It's over now, Livie. Go back to sleep," Theo said, pulling her closer to him.

Quinn and Jack slowly left the room and Theo held Livie until she was calm and had fallen back to sleep.

Theo hoped she would forget about her nightmare but he knew she wouldn't. Her sleep was too restless all night and when she woke in the morning, the dark circles rimming her eyes gave evidence of her restless sleep.

"HOW ARE YOU feeling?" Theo asked her for the hundredth time that morning.

"I'm fine. I'm marveling at the progress the ladies are making with the jams and jellies. Isn't this amazing, Theo?"

Livie looked out over the tables of jars of blackberry, blueberry and raspberry jams, and felt such an immense sense of accomplishment. They'd even picked enough strawberries to make a sizeable batch of strawberry jam. And it wasn't even noon, yet.

"Yes, this is absolutely amazing," Theo said. "At this rate, we'll have enough jams and jellies by the end of the week to make a trip to London and open our store before schedule."

"Oh," Livie said on a sigh as she filled another jar and sealed it. Then she took a damp cloth and wiped the jar to remove any stickiness. When it was cool, she would write what kind of jam was in the jar and put it in the correct box. "And the ladies said they'd come again tomorrow to finish up the fruit the children had picked."

"That's amazing," Theo said when Jack came in the kitchen door carrying two more baskets of raspberries.

"Aren't you running out of raspberries yet?" one of the ladies teased him when he set the berries down in front of them.

"Ha! You can't even tell we made a dent in the raspberry

bushes."

"Oh!" the ladies chorused on a laugh.

"And the vicar just came with some volunteers from the town. They're going to keep you ladies on your toes."

"Is my Willie among the men picking berries?" one of the ladies asked on a laugh.

"Yes," Jack answered. "I think I heard the vicar call out to a Willie."

"He'd better be. I told him he hadn't done a lick of work to help me take care of our own children from the day we got married ten years ago. The least he can do is help the children at the orphanage."

And so the day went. The men, women and children worked non-stop from morning to dusk then they went home and returned the following morning. By week's end, they had enough cases of jams and jellies to fill the back of the wagon and more.

"Are you going to go with us to London?" Theo asked Jack when they had the wagon loaded and were ready to start their journey.

"Yes, I'll go with you. You'll need help unloading these boxes when you get to London."

"How about you, Quinn?"

"I'm going to go with you but I'll leave you when you get close to Rosemont and visit my family for a few days."

"That's a wonderful idea, Quinn," Livie said. "You've been away from your family long enough. It's time you returned to them. We can manage setting up the shop without you."

"We'll see you in a couple of weeks. In time for our grand opening," Theo said.

"Are you going to bring your wife with you?" Livie asked. "I'd love to meet her."

"Yes," Quinn answered. "I think she'll need a break from the children by then."

"That sounds wonderful."

Livie was more excited than she'd been in ages. She was

going to go to London and with the profits from the jams and jellies, she would be able to purchase some of the items the children needed. First on her list would be some new books for the schoolrooms and the library. She couldn't wait to go shopping.

"You look happy," Theo said when he came up beside her.

"I am. I am very happy. And I owe it all to you, Theo. You're the one who came up with the idea of opening a shop in London."

"But you made it a reality."

"Do you have everything we'll need for our journey?" Livie asked when she looked at the back of the packed wagon.

"Yes, everything's ready to go."

"We'll leave first thing in the morning, then." Livie reached for Theo's hand and squeezed his fingers.

"Yes. First thing in the morning."

Excitement was building and nothing was going to put a halt to it. This was the most exciting day of her life and nothing was going to dampen her happiness.

⇛⇜

THE WEATHER WAS perfect for their journey to London. They started off as soon as it was light enough to travel with Theo driving the wagon and Quinn and Jack riding beside it. Four of the older boys rode in the back of the wagon. They would help unload the wagon and carry the cases of jams and jellies into the shop. In a few days, four of the older girls would come to work in the store. Livie was going to find someone to manage the store before they came. She had several possibilities in mind. These were girls who had lived at the orphanage and took positions in London when they got old enough. There were two in particular who she thought would be perfect to manage *Angel's Jams and Jellies*.

She couldn't believe how everything had fallen in line. It was as if everything had happened the way it was meant to.

They reached the turnoff where Quinn was to leave them and travel on to Rosemont. Theo decided this was a perfect place to stop and have lunch before they continued on to London.

"I'll see you in a week or two," Quinn said, then turned his horse toward Rosemont.

"Bring your wife with you," Livie reminded him before he went too far. "I want to meet the paragon of virtue who can put up with you and five children."

"What's only five children," Quinn countered. "You put up with more than twenty and live to tell it."

"That's true, isn't it?" Livie answered. "We are quite remarkable, aren't we?"

"Yes, you are," Quinn answered and rode on to Rosemont.

"Boys," Livie instructed them, "get the baskets of food out of the wagon and set them out on the side of the road. There's a blanket in there for us to sit on."

The boys did as they were instructed and Livie grabbed a bucket from beneath the seat. "I hear rushing water. There must be a stream nearby. I'll get some water and be right back."

"I'll go with you," Theo said. "I need to water the horses."

"Very well," Livie said, then waited for Theo to unhook the horses.

The stream wasn't too far away and they reached it in no time.

Livie walked beside Theo until they reached the stream. The day was sunny and bright and Livie let her gaze take in Theo's magnificent physique. He saw her watching him and lowered his gaze and blessed her with a smile that warmed her insides. She loved him. It was remarkable how deeply she loved him. She lifted the corners of her mouth to give him a broad smile, then her smile faded when she experienced a sharp pain in her arm.

"Livie!" Theo yelled, then rushed to Livie's side and pushed her down in the grass and covered her body. "Boys, get down!"

Theo yelled. "Jack!"

Theo lifted Livie in his arms. His hand came away warm and wet. "Don't move, Livie. You've been hit."

"Jack!" Theo cried out again and Jack came up beside him.

"Where'd the shot come from?"

"From the right," Theo said and Jack took off running in the direction of the gunfire.

A few moments later, Quinn rode up to them. "I heard a shot," Quinn yelled, then jumped from his horse and knelt beside Livie. "How badly is she hurt, Theo?"

"I'm fine, Theo," Livie moaned, holding her arm. "Go after him."

"I'm not leaving you," he answered, handing the bucket to Quinn.

Quinn ran to the stream and filled it.

Theo tore her sleeve and looked at the wound. "I've got to get the bleeding stopped," he said, wetting a clean handkerchief and pressing it against Livie's arm. "It's not bad," he said. "The bullet came out clean."

"I told you."

"So you did. But you won't be doing any heavy lifting for a while."

Theo held her in his arms and pressed the cloth against her wound. It wasn't overly bad, just bleeding a lot. He washed the wound and wrapped a cloth around her arm, then insisted that she rest for a few moments.

Theo looked up and saw Jack riding back. "Did you find him?"

"No. I lost him. He had too big of a head start on me. How badly is she hurt?" he said looking down on Livie.

"Not badly at all," Livie answered for herself. "It's just a scratch."

"You won't say that when it starts to hurt," Theo said.

"Was that McBride?" Livie asked. She wanted to believe Theo had been wrong when he said McBride wouldn't give up until she was dead. She wanted to think he would get as far away from her as possible, but obviously his hatred and bitterness was too great. He had no intention of letting her live.

"Yes, it was McBride," Theo answered.

"He isn't going to give up, is he?"

"No, Livie. He isn't."

Theo brought her up against him and held her for a few moments, then he scooped her up into his arms and carried her back to the wagon. He ordered the boys to get out the basket of food and eat, then he placed the blankets in the back and settled Livie on a blanket.

"Do you want something to eat?" Theo asked.

"No. I'm not hungry, but I would like something to drink. Something strong."

"Yes, you deserve it," Theo said with a smile. He took out a bottle of wine Mrs. Barnes had packet in the basket and poured some into a glass. "Drink all of it, Livie. It will help with the pain."

She did, and Theo filled it again.

When they'd finished eating, Quinn came up to Theo. "Do you want me to travel to London with you?" he asked.

"No. You want to get home and we're just shy of three hours from London. "Thanks, Quinn. I'm just glad you were close enough to hear the shots."

"After our years in the war, that's one sound you never forget."

"That's for sure," Theo said. "Willie," Theo said to one of the older boys. "Pack everything and let's get on our way."

"Yes, Captain Dunworthy."

"I'll see you in London in a couple of weeks," Quinn said and rode off. Jack checked the wagon to make sure everything was secure.

"I'll ride on ahead," Jack said. "We don't want any more surprises."

"No, we don't," Theo answered then went to the back of the

wagon to check on Livie.

"Your wine had its desired effect. I have a feeling I'm going to sleep all the way to London."

"Good. That will be the best thing for you. One of the boys will ride back here with you and the rest will ride up front with me."

Livie watched as the boys climbed aboard the wagon and they continued on their way to London.

It would take them several hours to reach London and another hour to find the location Quinn had purchased for their shop. When they reached the building where the Angel's Wing's Jams and Jellies was located, Theo could make a bed that Livie could sleep on.

Tomorrow would be a better day. At least, hopefully her arm wouldn't hurt so badly. If only their troubles would disappear.

If only the man who wanted her dead would go away and never come back.

CHAPTER EIGHTEEN

T HEY ARRIVED AT the address that Quinn had given them and Livie couldn't believe her eyes. The location was perfect. The interior of the shop was perfect. Everything about the new home of Angel's Wings Jams and Jellies was perfect. Even the surrounding shops were ideal.

"Are you pleased?" Theo asked her when he helped her inside.

"Oh, Theo. I couldn't be more pleased. It's perfect. And the ladies Quinn hired to clean the shop and dust the shelves did an amazing job."

"Yes, they did," Jack agreed. "It's clean enough that we can just move in and set up shop." Jack walked to the front door and looked down the street. "And we're very close to what looks like a popular restaurant. It's called Annie's Eatery."

"Are you hungry again, Jack?" Livie teased. "We just ate."

"No, I just thought we might want to make up a basket of our jams and jellies and leave it for them to try. Annie's might be our first customer."

"That's a remarkable idea," Livie said. "I think we should all stop by for lunch."

"Perhaps we can do that tomorrow," Theo chimed in, "but right now Livie needs to rest, and I need to tend to her arm. Her *scratch* is starting to bleed again."

"And the lads and I need to unload the wagon," Jack said, gathering the boys and leading them outside.

Theo went outside and brought the blankets back inside. He placed them on the floor and made a bed for Livie to sleep on.

"Lay down, Livie. You're as pale as a sheet."

"I do feel as though I need to close my eyes for a moment."

"Do you need me to get a doctor?"

"No, Theo. It's just a scratch, remember?"

"Yes, but we'll need to keep an eye on that scratch so it doesn't get infected. Which means no work for you for the next couple of days."

"Oh, but there's so much to do."

"Then you can stay where you are and point your finger and Jack and I and the boys can do what needs to be done."

Livie looked at Theo while he cleaned her arm and smiled at him. Without even looking to see who might be close enough to see them, Theo leaned down and kissed her. Her heart swelled in her breast.

She'd known when she first met him that he was special, but she didn't realize just how special he was. She did now and didn't ever want to lose him.

"How soon do you think it will be before we can open?" Theo asked her. He'd finished cleaning her wound and was putting on a clean bandage.

"A week," Livie said. "I want to go to the home where we send our girls when they get ready to train for domestic work and find three or four girls Mrs. Worth thinks would be good fits for working in our shop. Then, we need to make a sign that will go over the door. The sooner people see that we're getting ready to open, the sooner we'll have our first customers."

"Can you draw up what you want?"

"Marie helped me make up a design for the sign that will go above the door, and another that will hang inside. There are several smaller signs that can be put in the windows and on the shelves with all the names of the jams and jellies on them. They're all out in the wagon. We just need to find an artist who can make up what we need."

"I'll have Jack measure the size we'll need for over the door and find someone to make it."

"Oh, Theo. It's coming together. Our shop is coming together."

"Yes, it is, Livie. Now, close your eyes and get some rest. I need to go out and help the boys carry in the jams and jellies."

Livie let her gaze focus on Theo and she smiled at him. Her eyes closed and she was asleep.

Maybe this time she would have pleasant dreams instead of the nightmares that had plagued her for the last several weeks.

THEO AND JACK and the boys carried in box after box of jams and jellies. By late afternoon they had the wagon unloaded and stopped to rest. Livie still slept on the makeshift bed he'd placed in the corner behind a door that opened to the back room.

When Jack and the boys complained that they were hungry and wanted to get something to eat, Theo was tempted to wake her, then decided she needed the rest more than anything. His plan was to take his workers to Annie's Eatery and bring Livie back something when they returned. He thought that would be a perfect opportunity to introduce himself to the owners and present them with a jar of one of their jams.

"What's your favorite jam," he asked Jack and the boys.

"The raspberry jam," Jack said.

"The blackberry," one of the boys said.

"Strawberry," another boy said.

"The blueberry," another said.

Theo looked at them in disbelief. "Since you can't decide which one, I get to choose. It's the strawberry."

They laughed and Theo grabbed a jar of strawberry jam as they headed out the door. Before he left, he walked to the back and checked on Livie.

"We're going out to eat, Livie. We'll be back in a short while."

Theo smiled when she didn't answer. She was really tired. He was glad he'd made the decision to let her rest instead of waking her. He left the Angel's Wing's Jams and Jellies and caught up with Jack and the boys before they entered Annie's Eatery.

They arrived in the middle of the lunch rush and the eatery was so full they had to wait for a table.

Theo watched the young lads he had with him and realized that this was obviously the first time any of them had eaten in a restaurant. Their eyes were wide as saucers and they watched every platter that came from the kitchen with mouths drooling with anticipation.

Finally, they were shown to a table. As soon as they were seated, Theo asked to see the owner. An attractive lady approached their table. She was wearing a stiff black uniform and a white ruffled apron.

"Good day, gentlemen. My name is Annie. You asked to see me?"

"Yes." After Theo introduced himself and Jack, he explained that their shop was just down the street from them and their products were jams and jellies made at The Angel's Wing's Orphanage and Foundling Home. He then explained that all profits from the sale of the jams and jellies would go to providing food and clothing for the children there.

Several of the surrounding tables heard him speaking with Annie and asked when their shop would be open. Theo told them The Angel's Wings Jams and Jellies would open within the week, and they all professed an interest in their jams and jellies.

Theo then presented Annie the jar of strawberry jam he'd brought with him and opened it and to Theo's surprise, she handed out samples to all the interested patrons. The excitement was contagious and Theo wished Livie had been there to experience it. He considered going back to get her, but knew if she was sleeping, the rest would do her much more good.

Theo and Jack helped the young boys order their meals, then

they leisurely ate some of the most delicious food any of them had had in forever.

It was getting dark before they left Annie's Eatery and walked back to The Angel's Wings Jams and Jellies. Theo couldn't wait to tell Livie about their exciting evening.

⟫⟩⟩⟨⟨⟨

LIVIE OPENED HER eyes and tried to figure out exactly where she was. It took her several moments to remember that she was in London and had come with Theo and Jack and the oldest boys at the orphanage to bring the jams and jellies Mrs. Barnes and the volunteers from the church had made for them to sell at their new shop.

Livie sat up and stretched her arms and back. She was stiff and sore from laying on the blanket for so long. And her arm still hurt where a bullet had gone into her flesh.

She looked around the room, then rose to her feet. She was in the back room and she was alone.

"Theo?" she called out, but no one answered. "Theo," she called out again. When no one answered her second call, Livie walked from the back room where she'd been sleeping and went into the main shop area.

"Theo?" she called out a third time.

"Are you searching for someone, Mrs. Matthews?" a familiar voice asked.

Livie knew immediately who was speaking to her. She'd heard that voice often enough in her nightmares. She could put a face to that voice even though it was getting dark.

"What are you doing here?" she asked, trying to separate herself from her nemesis.

"Why, I've come to see you, of course."

"Well, I don't want to see you. You disgust me."

"That's not very hospitable of you. I hope you don't treat all your customers so poorly or you won't have many who return."

"Get out," she said, taking another step away from him.

"Don't you want to see what I've brought you?"

"I don't want anything you have."

"Oh, I think you'll want this," McBride said, then took one threatening step toward her and another. When he was dangerously close to her, he reached behind him and roughly pulled out a small lad. It was Jamie.

"No," Livie yelled. "Leave him be. Don't you hurt him."

Livie watched McBride roughly pull Jamie out from behind him and anchor him in front of him, far enough from Livie that she couldn't reach him even if she tried.

McBride glared at her with piercing hatred. "What? Are you afraid you will lose something important to you, like I lost everything that was important to me?"

"Mama."

"Let him go," Livie said, taking a step toward Jamie. She had to do whatever she could to save Jamie. She couldn't let anything happen to him.

Before she could get to her son, McBride pulled out a gun and pointed it at Jamie's temple.

"No!" she yelled. "Don't hurt him. He hasn't done anything to you."

"Just as I hadn't done anything to you, bitch, but you still took everything away that I'd worked so hard to have. All I wanted was to live my life in luxury and you took that away from me. The jewel was within my grasp and you gave it away."

"The jewel wasn't yours."

"Yes, it was! It was mine. I'm the one who took it in the first place. I was the one the French promised to make rich if I gave it to them. And then that bastard Wallace stole it away from me."

"So, you killed him to get it back."

"But he wouldn't die. Instead, he lived long enough to give it to you and you gave it back to the French. Damn you! You ruined everything!"

Livie looked around her and searched for anything she could use to defend herself. There was nothing. Theo hadn't left his gun in case she needed it. But why would he? He hadn't expected McBride to try to kill her twice in the same day.

"Just go," she said. "If you leave now, you'll have time to get away before they catch you. You can go to the Americas. You'll be safe there."

"Fool! I need money to go anywhere and you made sure I would never have any money. I have nothing now except what I want from you."

"What do you want from me?" Livie asked.

"Oh. What a silly question. Surely you know. I've come to kill you. You've ruined everything I've worked for my whole life. I could have had it all. The jewel was the answer to everything and the French were going to pay me for it. And then you gave it to them and demanded nothing in return."

McBride swung his pistol through the air and Livie feared Jamie would get hit with it. She feared that the gun would fire and Jamie wouldn't be able to get out of the way and would be hit.

"I killed for it. I betrayed my country for it, and in less than the blink of an eye, you took it all away from me."

"Then you can have me. You can kill me if that's what you want. Just let the boy go. He's not involved in this."

"Isn't he? I definitely think he is. I think if I have to give up everything that is important to me, you should have to give up everything that's important to you."

"No! Let him go. He's just a child!"

"No, bitch! You can watch him die like I watched my dreams die."

And just that fast, McBride aimed the gun at Jamie. Livie grabbed the only thing within reach, a jar of jam, and threw it at McBride. The jar hit him in the forehead and he lost his balance and fired the gun.

Livie felt a stinging sensation that caused her shoulder to burn like it was on fire.

"Livie!" a voice called out and Theo burst into the room with his gun aimed at McBride. He fired at the man who'd tried to kill her more than once today. When McBride didn't go down, Theo fired a second time, and this time, McBride fell to the floor.

"Jamie!" she cried out and rushed to her son. She wrapped him in her arms and held him close to her.

"Mama," Jamie called out and wrapped his arms around her trembling body. "Mama, you're hurt!"

"No, Jamie. I'm fine. I'm fine. Are you alright?"

"Yes, but you're bleeding."

"It's nothing, sweetheart. Nothing." But Livie knew it wasn't nothing. Her shoulder burned like it was on fire, just like her arm had earlier this afternoon. Only this time it hurt worse.

"Livie," Theo said, rushing to her. "You're hurt. Sit down here and let me see how badly."

"It's nothing, Theo. Just a scratch."

"You and your scratches." Theo gathered her in his arms and led her to a stack of boxes. He sat her down and opened the back of her gown to look at her wound.

"It's just a scratch, Livie, but this scratch is a little more severe than the scratch this afternoon."

By now, the shop was packed with onlookers. "Does anyone know where we can find a doctor?" Theo yelled.

"I do," a young man called out. "I'll go for him right now."

"Thank you," Theo answered. "Jamie," he said to his son. "Come and hold your mama's hand until the doctor comes. I have to talk to Uncle Jack a minute."

"I'll stay with the lad," the owner of Annie's Eatery said, stepping in to hold Livie steady. "My, my," she said, keeping Livie from falling over. "You sure do know how to make an impressive entrance into London."

Livie tried to smile but it was difficult. Her shoulder hurt too badly.

Just then, the doctor entered and took her to the back room. He chased Theo and Jamie out and only let Mrs. Mackey, the owner of Annie's Eatery, stay. He told Mrs. Mackey what he needed and before she came back with what the doctor wanted, Livie had closed her eyes and the room had gone dark.

⁕

CHAPTER NINETEEN

"H E'S DEAD," JACK told Theo when the doctor was tending to Livie.

"Good. Then this is finally over."

"Yes."

"Are you all right, Jamie?" Theo asked his son.

Jamie nodded. "That was exciting. You should have seen Mama. She's the bravest person in the whole world! She picked up a jar from the counter and threw it right at him. She hit him square in the forehead."

"She's quite something, Jamie, isn't she?"

"Yes, she is."

"Just remember that the next time you misbehave," Jack said with raised eyebrows. "If she decides she needs to throw something at you, don't think she'll miss."

The look on Jamie's face turned serious. "I won't."

Theo turned his attention to Jamie. "How did he get you?"

"I was out picking berries. You should have seen how many berries I picked. I got a whole basketful all by myself."

"That's good," Jack said. "The way your mama smashes the jars we'll need to replace them."

"Go on, Jamie," Theo urged.

"Anyway, that man rode up and grabbed me and brought me here."

"Did anyone see that you were taken?"

"Yes, Frank did. He chased us but the man's horse was faster than Frank's horse and it wasn't long and I couldn't see Frank following us any longer."

"We'll have to send word back to the orphanage that Jamie's with us and he's safe. And, that McBride is no longer a threat."

"I'll go first thing in the morning," Jack said. "I'll take the wagon and return with more jams and jellies."

"I'm sure there will be a few other items we'll need that we didn't think of before we left," Theo said.

"Make a list and I'll bring the items you need back with me. What about Jamie? Do you want him to go back with me?"

"No," Theo said. "I want him to stay with us. Livie will want him close for a while and I'll need him to make sure his mama stays in bed and gets plenty of rest. How does that sound, Jamie?"

"That sounds good. I don't want to leave my mama again. I was kind of scared of that man."

"I don't blame you," Theo said. "I would have been afraid, too."

"You would have?" Jamie asked.

"Absolutely. He wasn't a very nice man, was he?"

"No."

Just then, the doctor came out of the back room and walked toward them.

"How is she?" Theo asked as soon as the doctor came close enough.

"Lucky, sir. I took a look at her other wound. Whoever took care of it did a fine job, but she's going to need special care for a while. Having been shot twice on the same day isn't something the normal woman can survive and still do a regular day's work. She's going to need plenty of bedrest. And lots of water. And as much food as you can get down her. She looks like she hasn't been eating regular meals for a while."

"She hasn't. But we'll make sure she does now." Theo looked at Jamie. "Did you hear that, son? Your job will be to make sure your mama gets lots of sleep and plenty to eat and drink."

"I will, Da. I will."

"I know you will. Now, would you go pick out a jar of jam and a jar of jelly for the doctor?"

Jamie search through the boxes to find the jam and jelly he wanted to give the doctor while Theo gave the doctor some money for tending to Livie. "Are you sure she's going to be all right?"

"Yes, she's a strong lady, but I'd make sure she doesn't experience any more tragedies. Her body has taken enough punishment for now."

"I'll make sure she doesn't," Theo answered the doctor. "Thank you," he said, then looked to the door as the doctor left only to see Commander Waterford enter.

"Captain Dunworthy. Major Washburn. Please accept my apology for what Mrs. Matthews has gone through. Commander McBride had us all fooled."

"Who is he really?" Theo asked.

"His name is Paul Lamont. He was a Major in Her Majesty's army but was dishonorably discharged for several crimes including insubordination, failure to follow orders, theft and a list of other offenses as long as your arm. Somehow he discovered the real Commander Jason McBride was going to meet with Wallace at The Angel's Wings Orphanage and Foundling Home so he impersonated him in order to take possession of the papers and the jewel. He didn't care about the papers, but he was after the jewel. He knew the French would pay handsomely to get their jewel back and he was after the money."

"He shot Wallace when he was leaving with the jewel," Theo said, filling in the gaps of the story. "But Wallace made it to the orphanage and gave the jewel to Livie before he died."

"Yes, and he told Mrs. Matthews not to give the jewel and the papers to anyone other than Jason McBride."

"Livie asked what Jason McBride looked like and Wallace told her he had a scar on his face," Theo said. "That's when Livie realized Lamont wasn't the real McBride. She refused to hand over the jewel and gave it back to the French in exchange for not only the lives of the children, but our lives, too."

"After that, it was just hatred on his part because Mrs. Matthews had spoiled his chance to become a very rich man."

"Is the real McBride dead?" Jack asked.

"No. Lamont shot him and left him for dead, but he survived. He's still recovering from his wounds."

"Good," Theo said. "Enough people were hurt because of him."

"Yes, but there won't be any more, thanks to you, Captain."

"Not just me," Theo said. "Livie got to him first with a jar of preserves."

Waterford laughed. "I'll be sure to put that down on my report. Cause of death – Jar of Raspberry Preserves."

"That's fitting," Theo said finding that humorous.

"I'll get Lamont's body out of here. Thanks again for helping us get rid of Lamont."

Waterford turned and left, then Theo went to the back to check on Livie. He also needed to tell her that Jack was going back to the orphanage and wanted to know if she needed him to bring anything back with him.

When he got to where she was laying, he stopped and looked down on her. Jamie was snuggled beside her wrapped in her arms. They were both fast asleep.

He turned and went back to the main room and got everyone settled for the night. He would stand guard this first night, thankful that this should finally be an uneventful night.

⇒⟫⟪⇐

LIVIE OPENED HER eyes and looked about the room. It still took her several moments to remember where she was. It had been a week since she'd been shot. Theo had insisted that she be moved to a hotel with Jamie as her guard. Who knew a four-year-old could be so commanding. It was just another trait her son had inherited from his father – his sense of following the orders his commanding officer – his father – had issued.

Livie's week was up today and she couldn't wait to be able to go to The Angel's Wings Jams and Jellies. She knew, of course, that Theo wouldn't allow her to do any physical work, but at least she could issue orders and tell the three girls she'd chosen to work in the shop what she wanted done.

Thankfully, Theo had taken her to the Jelly Shop, as she was prone to calling it for short, several times during the week to keep up with the progress they were making to get the shop ready to open. And today, Quinn and his wife, Cassie, were scheduled to arrive. Livie couldn't wait to meet her. She knew, just from listening to Quinn talk about her, that Cassie was an exceptional woman.

Livie paced her hotel room in agitation, then stopped in front of Jamie. "Jamie, go get your father. If we don't leave soon the day will be over."

"No, it won't, mama. The sun's not all the way over the horizon."

"Well, it will be by the time your father gets here."

"Did I hear my name being disparaged?" Theo said, stepping into the room.

"I don't know, Da. What does dispardidged mean?"

"It means your mama was saying things about me that weren't very complimentary."

"Yup, she was," Jamie said, nodding in agreement. "You were being dispardidged."

"That's what I thought," he answered, then walked over to her and kissed her. "Good morning, sunshine," he said, and kissed her again. "Are you ready to get something to eat?"

"I'd like to go to the Jelly Shop first," Livie said.

"But I'm hungry," Jamie complained.

"You can have a bun when we get to the shop," Theo told his

son. "I got some for the workers and there might be one left if we hurry."

"Let's go, then," Jamie said, leading the way out the door.

They walked to the shop and when they arrived, Livie stepped inside the room and halted her steps like she always did when she first entered. "Oh, Theo. This is amazing."

"Yes, it is, Livie. Jack returned last night with another wagon of supplies and there were several cases of orange marmalade in the wagon."

"Wonderful." Livie turned to Theo. "Oh, do you think we're going to have to change our name to The Angel's Wings *Jams and Jellies and Marmalade?*

Theo laughed. "No, Livie. We can't change our name every time we add a product. Soon enough, we won't have room on our sign to add any more words. And I've come up with another item we need to add to our jams and jellies."

"What?"

"Honey. Angel's Wings Honey!"

"Oh, Theo. That is a wonderful idea. We'll add that as soon as we can."

Livie kissed Theo on the cheek, then took time to walk around the room, admiring all the displays the girls had set up around the shop. She made sure all the signs were easy to see and read. When she was satisfied that everything was ready for their Grand Opening tomorrow, she breathed a sigh of relief. This is what would make the orphanage and foundling home self-sufficient. This is what would feed and clothe the children who had no one else to care for them. This is what would enable them to take in more children than they were able to care for now. And it might even enable them to open a second Angel's Wings Orphanage, and a third.

Livie couldn't explain the emotions churning inside her. Suddenly, without bidding them to appear, huge tears spilled from her eyes and ran down her cheeks.

"What's wrong, Livie?" Theo asked, wrapping his arms

around her and holding her tight. "Are you all right?"

"Yes," she blubbered, "I'm fine. I'm just… happy."

"Oh," Theo said with a frown on his face.

"What's wrong?" Jack asked, coming over to see what was the matter.

"Nothing," Theo said shrugging his shoulders. "She's just happy."

"Happy?" Jack asked, looking at Theo with a confused expression. "Next time you get this happy, Livie, could you dance a jig, or sing a bawdy song? That way we'll know everything's all right."

"I'll remember that," Livie said, wiping the tears from her eyes.

"What's wrong?" Quinn asked from the door when he and his wife entered. "Did something else happen?"

"No, sweetheart," Quinn's wife, Cassie said coming over to greet Livie. "Those are tears of happiness. You men are going to have to learn to tell the difference."

Cassie hugged Livie and greeted her like a long-lost sister. After they'd spent a few moments getting to know each other, Livie showed Cassie around the shop. By the time they were acquainted, Livie knew she'd found one of the best friends she'd ever have in Quinn's wife, Cassie. It had been so long since she actually felt a connection to another woman her age, tears welled in her eyes.

"Are you happy again?" Theo asked.

"Yes, very." Livie smiled with happiness when he stepped toward her.

"I have a surprise for you," he said.

"What?" she asked.

Theo reached into his pocket and removed a folded sheet of paper. Livie simply looked at it when he handed it to her.

"Take it Livie. It's for you. Well, actually for us."

Livie took the paper and unfolded it. "Oh, my, Theo," she said in a breathless voice. "Really?"

"Yes, really. If you'll accept."

"Of course I accept."

"What is it, Mama? What does the paper say?"

"It says your Father wants to marry me."

A loud round of applause filled the Jam and Jelly Shop and Theo took her hand and they stood before a man Livie hadn't noticed had entered the shop.

"This is Reverend Cavanaugh. He said he'd marry us as soon as you gave him the paper you're crushing in your hand."

"Oh," she squeaked, handing him the special license.

Reverend Cavanaugh married Theo and Livie, and Livie cried through the ceremony. Then, he pronounced them man and wife and they were legally married.

"Da?" Jamie asked.

"Yes, son?"

"Mama is really crying now. Are those happy tears or sad tears? I can't never tell."

"Oh," Theo answered pulling Livie into his arms and kissing her. "Those are happy tears. Very, very happy tears.

CHAPTER TWENTY

THE GRAND OPENING of The Angel's Wings Jam and Jelly Shop was a huge success. Even better than Livie had imagined.

They opened early and there were customers lined up at the door waiting to get in. Theo greeted them as they came inside, and from that moment on, there wasn't a span of more than five minutes where there weren't customers in the shop.

Livie couldn't hazard a guess as to which jam or jelly was the most popular, although they sold out of the strawberry jam and the orange marmalade.

The girls from the orphanage's training school did a remarkable job selling their product and answering the customers' questions. Quinn's wife, Cassie, more than anyone, seemed to be enjoying herself. She said it was because she'd been confined in the country with her five children for so long that she finally felt as if she was free.

Even Jack seemed to enjoy himself. Several of the husbands who came in with their wives were former army soldiers. Livie didn't know how he recognized them, since they weren't in their uniforms, but he did and he struck up a conversation with them immediately. That seemed to help sales. Those soldiers purchased more jams and jellies than Livie thought they'd intended just because of their connection.

And, of course, the stories of the orphans without parents

tugged at even the hardest of hearts. Livie was always available to tell their stories.

But the biggest moment of the day came when the owner and manager of the largest hotel in London walked through the doors. Livie had no idea who he was until he introduced himself, but he asked to sample the jams and jellies, and after tasting each one, placed a standing order for several cases every week to be delivered to the hotel's restaurant. That alone, guaranteed the success of The Angel's Wings Jams and Jellies.

Closing time finally came and Quinn and Cassie, Jack, Theo and Livie, and all of the workers were dead on their feet. Theo treated them all to a celebratory dinner at Annie's Eatery. That seemed to be everyone's favorite place to eat.

"What a day we've had," Livie said when they were all gathered around a large table in the private dining room at Annie's.

"Yes, it has been quite spectacular," Theo said, placing his arm around Livie's shoulders and bringing her close to him. "I especially liked the part before the shop doors opened."

"What happened then?" Jamie asked, as if nothing could compare to the rush of people that entered the shop when they first opened.

"The part where your Mama and Father got married," Jack said, gently shoving Jamie on the shoulder.

"Oh, yeah, that part."

"Yes, son," Theo said. "That part."

Everyone laughed.

"And you know what the best part of that is?" Jack said, talking to Jamie.

"No, what?"

"That means that you get to sleep in my room with me tonight."

"I do?" Jamie said, brimming with excitement.

"Yes, you do."

"Why do I get to sleep in your room and not with my mama and da?"

"Yes, Jack." Quinn said. "Would you care to explain that one to a four-year-old?"

"Well, it's very simple," Jack said, obviously searching for the right words. "It's because you and Uncle Jack get to sleep in as late as we want in the morning and eat breakfast at Annie's Eatery, while your Uncle Quinn and Aunt Cassie, and your mama and da have to get up very early and work at the jelly shop."

"All right!" Jamie said excitedly. "I like that."

"So do I," Jack said. "So do I."

"Then," Theo said. "After we close up tomorrow night, we're going to have to discuss what our next move will be. I know Quinn and Cassie can't stay in London forever."

"No," Cassie agreed, "not forever. But we can stay a little longer than just two days."

"I agree," Quinn answered. "I was thinking perhaps a week or so."

"That will be wonderful," Livie said. "I want to spend more time getting to know Cassie, and getting her input on any changes that need to be made to the shop."

"And I need to make a trip back to the orphanage," Theo said. "We have to get the rest of the jams and jellies. We need everything to be here, not taking up space at the orphanage."

"And I'm afraid that Jamie will have to go back, too," Livie said. He's missed out on enough school days."

"Ahh," Jamie complained.

"None of that, Jamie," Livie scolded. "You've had more adventures in this past week than any of your friends have had in their whole lives. Besides, I'm sure they can't wait to hear all about them."

"Yea," Jamie agreed. "They'll be so jealous. They'll wish it would have been them that mean, nasty McBride would have grabbed."

"And you have a lot of work waiting for you back at the orphanage," Livie reminded him. "There are a lot of berries that need to be harvested. You know, we have to get them all picked before the first frost. We can't leave them to rot on the vines."

"I know," Jamie agreed as if he were ten years older than his nearly five years.

Livie stepped closer to him and wrapped her arm around him. "Don't you grow up on me too fast, my little man."

"I won't, Mama. Grown-ups have to work too hard. I like being little."

Livie leaned down and kissed her son on the cheek.

"Don't, Mama. Everybody will see."

Theo stepped up beside Livie and kissed her on the cheek just like she'd kissed Jamie's. "Just wait until you get older, Jamie. Getting kissed by a beautiful lady is something you'll look forward to."

"Not me," Jamie said and everyone laughed. "I'll never like a lady kissing me."

"If only," Livie said. "At least for twenty years or longer."

"Only in your dreams, sweetheart," Theo said, then kissed his wife for real.

THE ANGEL'S WINGS Jam and Jelly Shop had been open for one whole week, and sales were still far beyond expectations. Theo and Livie had canvassed the area and found several shops that were eager to carry Angel's Wings Jams and Jellies as part of their stock. They also made a list of everything they needed to bring back from the orphanage. Livie was anxious to return. She hated to admit it, but for as much as she loved running her little shop, she loved working at the orphanage even more. She missed the children, but most of all, she missed the babies. Perhaps that was because she thought she might be having one of her own in about seven months. She couldn't be sure, of course. It was too soon to tell, but the signs were all there.

"Tonight when we close, we need to eat, then retire early.

Tomorrow is going to be a long day. And we want to say goodbye to Quinn and Cassie. They'll be leaving first thing in the morning, too."

"Do you feel comfortable with the manager you hired to take care of the shop?" Theo asked.

"Yes. She's doing an amazing job, and the girls we hired when we first opened can all step in if she needs help. Besides, Jack said he'd stay in London and oversee things until we returned."

"I'm going to take an inventory so we know exactly what we have on hand," Livie said, then went to the storeroom and started counting jars of jams and jellies. The time flew by and it was time to close.

"Let us treat you to a farewell dinner," Theo said to Quinn and Cassie and Jack, and they locked up and walked to Annie's Eatery. When they got there, Annie showed them to a small private dining room in the back.

"We'll take a bottle of your best wine, Annie."

"Very good, Captain Dunworthy. What is the occasion?"

"It's the end of a very good week, Annie, and Colonel Beckham and his wife will be leaving in the morning to return home, and my wife and I will be leaving to return to the orphanage. I'm afraid it will be much quieter here with all of us gone."

"Not that much quieter," Jack said. "I'll still be here, Annie. I'll do my best to keep things lively."

"I'll look forward to that, Major," Annie said, then left to get their wine.

They ate their meals, and Jamie fell asleep immediately after pudding. They had a final glass of wine, then Theo set down his glass. "I have a question, Quinn."

Quinn turned his attention to Theo.

"Do you miss it?"

"The work as a special agent, you mean?"

"Yes. Do you miss the assignments?"

Quinn slid his chair closer to Cassie's and wrapped his arm around her shoulders. "Honestly, no. I thought I would. In fact, I was terrified that I would. But I don't. When you wrote that you needed my help, my first reaction was that rush of excitement because I might be walking into danger. But as soon as that thought appeared, it left. I have five children and soon there will be one more."

Quinn and Cassie shared a look filled with emotion. "And Cassie has promised to just bless me with one baby this time instead of an entire platoon."

Everyone laughed as they offered their congratulations.

"The thought of leaving them to fend for themselves while I go on an assignment terrifies me. All I want to do from this day on is to raise my children and watch them grow. I cannot explain the satisfaction I get from that task. And believe me, it's not an easy task, as anyone with children will tell you."

Quinn paused for a moment. "Why, Theo? Are you considering giving up working for the Crown?"

"No, I'm not considering. I've already decided. Unlike you, Livie and I don't just have five children to take care of. We have upwards of twenty at any one time."

"And in a few months," Livie said, "we'll have one more to care for."

Livie smiled. It took Theo a minute to understand what she was telling him, but when he did, his face lit up as if he'd heard the greatest news in the world. He leaned over and wrapped her in an embrace, then brought his mouth down over hers.

"I hope you're happy about it, Theo. I'm not going to let you run out on me this time."

"And I won't. I'll never abandon you again." Theo kissed her again. "That confirms my decision. I'm finished doing any work for Her Majesty. From now on, I'll only be taking care of the children under my roof."

"That only leaves you, Jack," Quinn said, and everyone's attention turned to Jack.

"Don't look at me," Jack said. "I'm already married and I intend to remain blissfully separated from my adoring wife."

"What?" Cassie and Livie said in unison. "You are married?" Cassie said in bewilderment. "We didn't know that!"

"Well, now you do," Jack finished.

"What happened," Livie asked, "if you don't mind us asking?"

"Let's just say my wife and I decided that the only part of marriage we could agree on was that we couldn't stand each other and didn't want to be married to each other any longer."

Jack reached for his glass of wine and drank until it was empty. "Anyway, that's an old and very boring story. Thankfully, I have no commitments at the moment other than staying in London, supervising your shop by day and carousing various dens of iniquity by night. It promises to be a great time."

Jack's story put a pall on the evening. Theo reached for Livie's hand and squeezed her fingers, secretly telling her that he'd tell her about Jack's situation later, although Livie doubted Theo knew much about it. Jack didn't seem like the type to bare his soul to anyone. Even his closest friends.

"So," Jack continued, "how long do you anticipate being away from London?"

Quinn was the first to speak. "I'm not sure I can commit to traveling to London more than two or three times a year. Running an estate keeps me tied down."

"I'll be back more often," Theo said. "Probably once every other month for a week or so each time."

"Well, I'll be around should you need me," Jack said. "You can always count on me to fill in for you."

"Thank you, friend."

"It's my pleasure," Jack said then filled his wine glass and drank.

The group of friends bid each other a final goodbye, then parted for the night.

"What happened with Jack and his wife?" Livie asked when they were on their way back to the hotel and out of hearing.

"I'm not sure Jack even knows. One day they were madly in love. The next they hated each other. That was three years ago.

His wife left him and they haven't seen each other since."

"How sad," Livie said, thinking of how lonely Jack must be. "No wonder he finds consolation in the arms of every beautiful woman he meets."

"I think that's how he copes. Jack doesn't handle loneliness well."

"What do you think will happen to him, Theo? Do you think he'll ever find someone he can love?"

"I don't know, Livie. I just know I'm glad we found each other again."

Livie placed her arm through Theo's. He held a sleeping Jamie in one arm and her in the other. "I love you, Theo. Are you sure you will be happy with an orphanage filled with children?"

"Ha!" Theo laughed. "Of course I will. How could I not with you at my side. The love we have for each other is very special."

Theo stopped in the middle of the London walk and wrapped his arm around Livie and kissed her. "It's a love that knows no bounds, my love. A love that will last an eternity."

About the Author

Laura Landon taught high school for ten years before leaving the classroom to open her own ice-cream shop. As much as she loved serving up sundaes and malts from behind the counter, she closed up shop after penning her first novel. Now she spends nearly every waking minute writing, guiding her heroes and heroines to find their happily ever afters.

She is the author of more than a dozen historical novels, including SILENT REVENGE, INTIMATE DECEPTION, and her newest Montlake Romance release, INTIMATE SURREN-DER.

Her books are enjoyed by readers around the world.